Published by Samantha Sabian and Arianthem Press

THE RUNNER THIEF Vol 3 CHRONICLES OF ARIANTHEM, 2014. FIRST PRINTING.

Office of Publication: Los Angeles, California

THE RUNNER THIEF, CHRONICLES OF ARIANTHEM, its logo, all related characters and their likenesses are ™ and © and ™ 2014 Samantha Sabian and Arianthem Press.

What did you think of this book? We love to hear from our readers.

Please email us at: samantha@arianthem.com.

THE RUNNER THIEF

THE CHRONICLES OF ARIANTHEM III

SAMANTHA SABIAN

ARIANTHEM PRESS

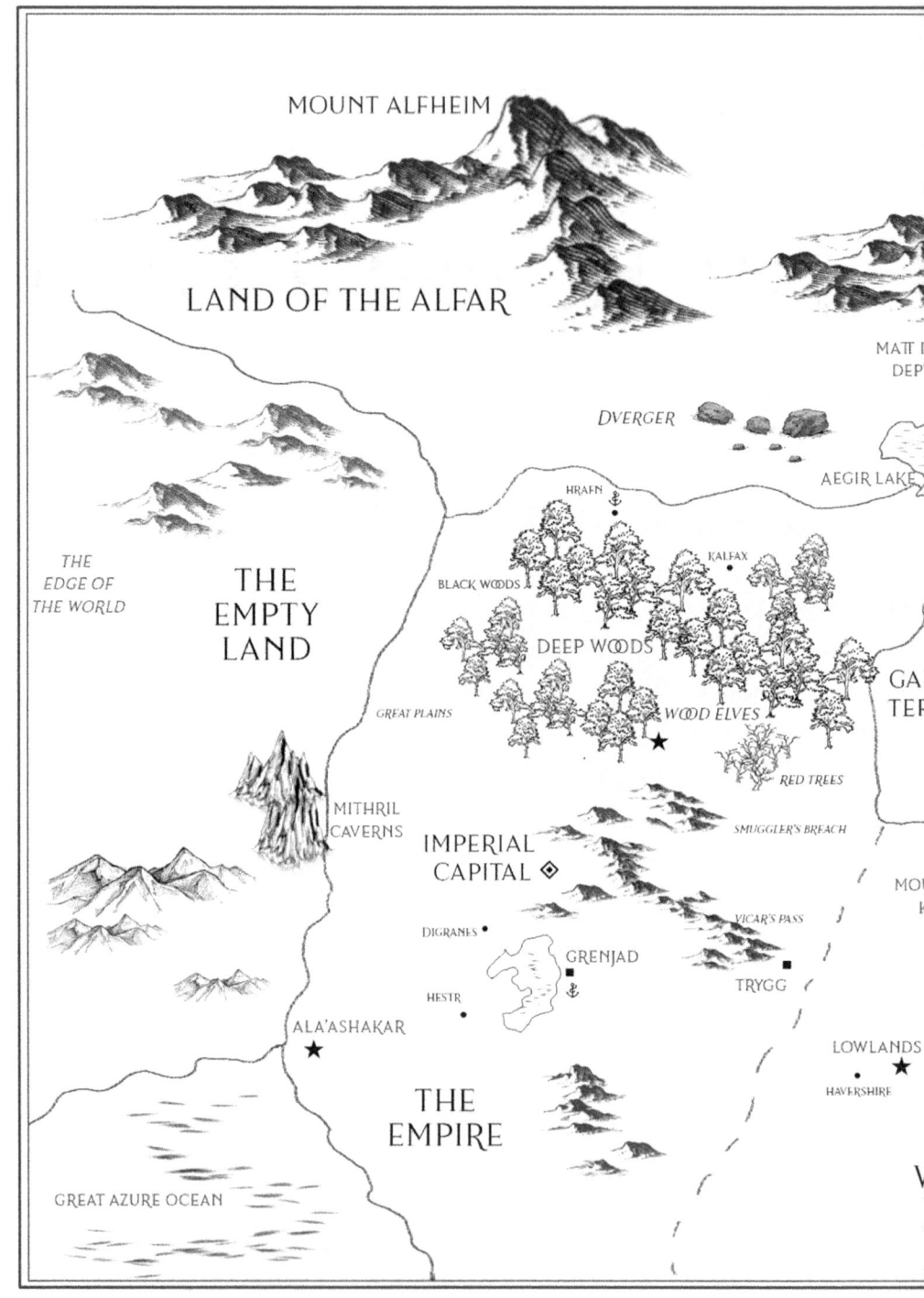

ONS

KYLAN'S
CASTLE
★

BALDUR'S PEAK

DARBY FALLS
REIST KEEP

DVERGER

TER
ORY

GUDRID •

HALDIS ◈

THE
SJOFN ACADEMY
★

LAND OF THE
HA'KAN

ARIANTHEM

CIRCA 312 AGW

CHAPTER 1

S yn watched the mark carefully. He was plump which meant that he was well-fed. His clothing was a trifle gaudy, expensive but lacking in any refinement or taste. That meant he was wealthy but probably not of nobility. He wore several rings on both hands and two gold chains about his neck. One appeared to have a ruby dangling from the end of it. That would be difficult, she mused, because the weight would be noticeable. The merchant also had a bulge at his waistline inside his robe that was likely a pouch.

A small boy, a street urchin, approached the merchant, holding out his hand for alms. The merchant's features twisted into arrogant distaste and he pushed the boy to the side, causing him to stumble and nearly fall. The look on his face would have been enough for Syn to act; the push merely sealed the merchant's fate.

Noma, celebrant of Sjöfn, watched the scene unfold from the doorway of the temple. She saw Syn, saw the merchant, and saw the merchant's base action toward the urchin. She sighed and stood upright from the doorway. She turned her back on the scene and went inside the temple to pray.

Syn pulled her hood over her head and pushed herself away from the wall she had been leaning against. She began meandering toward the merchant. She stopped to examine the various wares on display, showing particular interest in the fresh vegetables of the day. She picked up a nice healthy squash, then turned to get a better look at in the light. Unfortunately, she turned full on into the merchant, smacked him with the squash, then comically juggled it about his shirtfront in an attempt to keep from dropping it. It was to no avail, however, and the squash went to the ground as both the merchant and the vendor began soundly cursing her.

"I beg your pardon, sirs!" Syn cried, then accidently stepped on the squash, spraying juice onto the hem of the merchant's gown. She kneeled to wipe his robe, making the mess all the worse. The merchant snatched the hem from her grasp and sent a kick towards her, which she avoided.

"Get your hands from me!" the merchant said venomously. Syn stood up and backed away, hands raised upward as if in surrender. She bowed humbly in apology once more, then pivoted on her heel and disappeared into the crowd. She made a right turn into the first alley, then a left, then another right, heading down towards the docks. Her fence was there, the contact who would buy all her stolen goods. She patted her pocket; she had pilfered three of the five rings, the ruby necklace, and the pouch of gold. She would have to lay low for a while. She generally did not like to make such a scene, but that bastard had been asking for it and she could only have obtained one or two of the items by stealth. Instead, by flailing about, she was able to nearly clean him out. She would have to remember to pay the vendor for the squash.

Noma lit the candles one by one. Evening was falling and the smell of burning fireplaces was pleasant in the air. She kneeled before the altar of Sjöfn, praying for love and healing for all those in need. She rose to her feet and finished lighting the sconces, which cast gentle light onto the tiles of the temple. She turned to find Syn standing there. At one time, her silent presence would have caused Noma to start with fear, but she had grown used to the woman's noiseless movement.

"And do you have another gift of coin for the temple?"

Noma's tone of voice told Syn that the priestess knew whence the money had come.

"So, you saw," Syn said with resignation.

"No," Noma said angrily, her anger more from fear than judgment, "I couldn't watch. I came into the temple to pray."

Syn lifted the lid of the box that held the temple coffers and placed a large bag of gold within. She had given some to the urchin and kept enough for about a week's expenses, the rest she gave to the church.

"If you were praying for my soul, 'tis a waste of time," Syn said.

"I don't pray for your soul," Noma said, still angry, "I pray for your safety. You're reckless. If they catch you, they'll behead you."

Syn took the woman into her arms, enjoying the softness of her body. Noma struggled a bit, but not very much, and Syn kissed her. "They aren't going to catch me," Syn said.

Noma stared at the woman in front of her. Truly she had a soft spot in her heart for Syn. Syn was rakishly good-looking, not beautiful, but roguishly attractive. Her green eyes twinkled with good humor and a deviltry that melted the hearts of men and women alike. She was of medium height and athletic build which allowed her to pass as a man much of the time when hooded as she was today. When the disguise came off, her fine features were far more feminine although she probably still could pass as an elven male. Her dark brown hair was shoulder length, and oddly, when she pulled it back, she looked more male than when she wore it loose, as she did now, and the locks softened her face. Noma had teased her about being a shapeshifter, so uncanny was the ability.

"So, will you forgive me?" Syn asked, then kissed her again before she could respond. She took a step forward, her hands about Noma's waist, and

3

SAMANTHA SABIAN

Noma knew she was being maneuvered into the small side-room that held her bed.

"No," Noma said, her arms coming up around Syn as she passionately returned the kiss, "I will not forgive you."

Syn eased her backwards through the doorway, gave the door a gentle kick to close it, then pressed the priestess onto the bed. "Then allow me to do penance." She skillfully undid the buttons down the front of Noma's robes and parted the folds, still kissing the priestess. She pressed her knee gently but firmly between Noma's legs, causing the woman to moan with desire as she pulled her own overshirt from her head. She wore only a thin shift now and pressed herself to Noma's generous breasts, loving the softness against the firmness of her torso. She continued to kiss her, nibbling at her throat, then trailing a searing kiss down to the breasts where she took the fullness in her mouth with great pleasure. Syn loved women. She loved the way they looked, the way they smelled, the way they tasted. She loved the softness of their skin, the curves of their bodies, the warm wetness between their legs that she seemed gifted to bring forth. And women sensed that love even though it was not directed exclusively at them, and they fell into her arms and into her bed with abandon.

Syn's kiss moved lower until her mouth settled between Noma's legs and the priestess arched with need. The lips and tongue moved with marvelous skill and intuition. The fingers did their part as well, stroking firmly until the nun was entirely in her control and she drove the priestess to orgasm swiftly. Noma's last intelligible thought was that she hoped the temple was empty because she began crying out about "sin" quite loudly with no inhibition.

When the room was again silent, Syn pulled herself up onto Noma's softness, then rolled her over so the priestess lay in her arms. Noma felt very sated and content but, as always, a little guilty.

4

"Is there a reason why you won't allow me to give you pleasure?" Noma asked.

Syn looked down at her, grinning a little. "Could you not tell I enjoyed that?"

"That's not what I mean," Noma said. "You never allow me to bring you release."

"Hmm," Syn said, stretching, "You're a priestess and I'm a thief. All I do is take, and all you do is give. I think it right that I seek to balance that."

The answer did not satisfy her, but Noma settled into Syn's arms, and soon Syn's rhythmic breathing indicated she was fast asleep. Syn at times seemed so simple: a rogue, a rake, and a crook. But there were other times she seemed unutterably complex, like moments before when that humor could barely disguise a deep sadness in her eyes.

The next morning, Syn rose early. Noma was still asleep, and Syn took a long moment to examine her lovely, soft features. She knew her actions from the day before would have consequences: more guards, more vigilance, a bounty on her head were they to learn her identity. And such a large heist would attract the attention of the Guild who would not look kindly on such an unsanctioned theft by a non-member. She had enjoyed the time she had spent in this small village, and especially enjoyed her stint with Noma. But, like so many other times and so many other places and so many other women, Syn turned her back and walked away, knowing she would never see Noma or the town again.

CHAPTER 2

The caravan guards were well-armed and looked like they could handle themselves, but still, Syn was a little nervous. She was not good with a sword or bow, or really any weapon at all, so she liked to travel in the company of others. She would pay for the protection with ill-gotten gains, and sometimes even steal it back at the end of the trip depending on whether or not she had enjoyed her companions. But she did not like to travel with anyone who displayed any outward trappings of wealth; it attracted the wrong type of people, people like her, only more violent.

They were in three wagons, and most of the travelers were common folk, a farmer, a tailor and a couple of tradesmen. But there was one nobleman, or at least someone who wished to be seen as a nobleman. Syn guessed by his demeanor he had some minor pedigree that had seen better days. That didn't stop him from looking down his nose at everyone and ordering his servants about in a rude manner. What made it worse was that he most likely did not possess the wealth he intimated, so if the caravan was attacked, the robbers would be angry at the waste of time.

Even so, riding in the back of the gently rocking wagon was better than walking. It was not comfortable, but it was not crowded, and she could stretch out her legs. There were no other women in the group, so she was dressed as a man, her hair pulled back beneath her hood. She kept to herself, and her traveling companions did not seem to desire conversation, so it might be a pleasant enough trip. Her destination, Trygg, was a fair-sized town, and although it had an imperial garrison there, it seemed it might provide some work for someone with her skills. The Guild also had a presence there, which could be problematic, but she had dealt with that before. Trygg was a considerable ways, but Syn liked to put distance between herself and her past actions, well, those most recent, and as a result found herself traveling all over Arianthem.

At least there would be no Hyr'rok'kin, Syn thought. They had been seen only sporadically the last fifteen, twenty years, very few since the massive outbreak in her childhood. Syn quickly pushed this thought away; it was too painful. No, the worst thing they had to worry about would be bandits. The rocking of the wagon was soothing, and she began to get drowsy. It would be better for her to sleep during the day and stay alert at night when they stopped.

It was the third day of their journey when Syn's fears were realized. They were skirting the edge of a vast wilderness when raucous cries erupted from the surrounding rocks. A dozen men leaped out and a half dozen more stood on the ledge above and began raining arrows down upon them. Syn's survival instinct was far better than her companions and she went over the side of the wagon and beneath it. The horses reared, startled, then bolted. She grabbed the railings underneath the coach and managed to pull herself up to the bottom of the carriage as it careened out of control. The ground beneath her raced by at a dizzying speed, and she knew if she lost her grip and fell it would injure if not kill her. She was not strong in an absolute sense, but very strong relative to her size and she held tight. The only good thing about the situation was that the sounds of fighting were growing fainter.

Despite the bumping and jarring, Syn began to work her way to the front of the carriage. She nearly lost her grip as she sought to pull herself up onto the side, but she jammed her hand into the crack between the seat and carriage. It hurt terribly, but she was able to pull herself up onto the seat. The driver was dead, an arrow through his throat, but he still held the reins in his lifeless hands. Syn took the leather straps from the dead man and with immense effort brought the frothing, snorting horses to a halt.

She glanced back. The sound of the other two wagons under attack could still be heard, but that battle would not last long. She glanced to the seats in the rear of the open coach. Her traveling companions had not reacted as quickly as had she; the farmer and the tailor were dead. She went through their pockets, then through those of the driver. She found some coin, a few items of jewelry, a dagger, and some curatives that might come in handy. She felt no remorse over her thievery. These men were dead through no fault of hers, and the sound of approaching hoofbeats told her if she did not take the goods, the pursuing bandits would. She jumped from the side of the wagon, landed lightly, then sprinted to the nearby tree line. With great trepidation she entered the forest, a place that would conceal her, but one only slightly less dangerous than the robbers at her heels.

It did not seem that much time had passed, but Syn knew she was already completely lost. She was gifted in a city, able to traverse the twists and turns of the streets and alleys, disappearing into shadows, scaling walls, balancing on ledges, finding ways into shops and residences that seemed impenetrable. She could analyze a layout, a building, a courtyard, really, any man-made structure and find its strengths and weaknesses. She could find food in scarcity, warmth in the frigid cold, water in a drought. There was no lock she could not pick, no safe she could not break, no window or door that would not open for her.

Here, she thought grimly, here was another story. She would probably be dead within the hour. She was good in a brawl, a dirty hand-to-hand fighter, but that wasn't going to be much use if she ran into a bear. Almost any man would go down with a good kick to his groin. She wasn't even certain if bears had a "groin." And the dagger she had plucked from the farmer wouldn't do her much good as she had found she was a greater danger to herself than others when wielding most weapons.

Syn sighed. She had some hard biscuits and some dried venison with her, enough for one, maybe two meals, but after that it would be rough going. She knew nothing of plants and would likely poison herself if she tried to eat anything. The forest creatures were in no danger from her and even the smallest hare was probably laughing at her right now. She did know how to fish, so if she found a pond or a stream, she might be in luck. She sighed again and started walking.

It seemed as if days had passed, although Syn knew that wasn't true because the sun was just now going down for the first time since the caravan attack. The forest smelled so unnaturally fresh to her, all moist earth and pine needles, that the aroma of a campfire was assuredly a hallucination. She sniffed the air again. No, it was definitely a campfire, and the smell of cooking meat was mouth-watering. The hardtack and dried venison had been gone since noon and her stomach was growling. She followed the smell, her nose evidently her one sense that was willing to aid her in her current predicament.

She could see the light through the forest and crept quietly to the edge of a small clearing. The first thing that caught her eye was the rusty cage suspended from a large tree. That was a very bad sign, and she kept in hiding.

The second thing that caught her eye was the witch stirring some brew in a cauldron, and that was an even worse sign. Witches were unpredictable. This woman might greet her presence with disinterest, might tell her to go away, or she might paralyze her with some spell and then put her in that cage to eat her. If she had any sense at all, Syn thought, she should disappear back into the forest.

But the food smelled so good. Not good enough for her to chance revealing herself, but good enough for her to hide in the bushes until the witch went to sleep and Syn could steal it. And although Syn was restless in every part of her life, there was one arena in which she was utterly patient: the job. And right now, the job was to steal some food.

Syn settled in to watch the woman. The witch was plain, her features neither attractive nor unattractive. It was hard to tell what her body looked like beneath the rough-hewn robe she wore although Syn spent a great deal of time trying to see and imagine what those curves might be. It was how she often entertained herself, although in this particular instance it would have no follow-up at all. Finally, the witch disappeared into the small, tent-like structure and the campsite settled into silence.

Syn waited awhile longer, just to make sure, then slowly crept toward the campfire. She pulled the meat from the spit and stuffed it into her pockets. She would not risk eating here. She inspected the area to see if there was anything of value, then looked indecisively toward the tent. This is where she often battled herself, where that recklessness that Noma had chastised took over and made Syn attempt things that no sane person would. It wasn't that Syn was greedy; she gave away almost everything she stole. It was the excitement, the thrill, the challenge that drove her. It was the idea that she could take anything at will. It made her one of the most dangerous thieves in all of Arianthem, but it made her as dangerous to herself as others.

As usual, she lost the battle and crept toward the tent. She silently pushed her way through the flaps, crouching low until her vision adjusted to the dim light. There were two sleeping forms as there was a second witch asleep at the far side. Syn plucked several mysterious looking items from a knapsack, then a few potions from a nearby chest. A few pots and pans and some drying herbs were hanging from ropes strung across the top of the tent, but Syn had no interest in those. She examined a few scrolls, then took those as well. Junior mages and would-be wizards often had interest in such things and were willing to pay good coin for them.

Syn had made her way silently through the entire tent and thought she had taken everything of value. Neither of the witches had moved. The first one, the one who had been outside, had removed her robe but was now covered by a blanket. Syn fought the urge to lower the blanket to see if her speculation about the curves had been close. She turned her attention to the second and her eyes widened. This one was lying on her side, naked, only partially covered by a blanket. She was beautiful in a frightening sort of way and the nipples of the full breasts were almost visible above the blanket. Syn could feel her palm itch as she fought the compulsion to pull the blanket lower. She wrestled with herself, then finally won a battle as she stood to exit the tent.

Unfortunately, the breasts had so distracted her she won the battle but lost the war. She stood upright into one of the cast-iron pans, striking it with enough force that she knocked herself out cold.

Syn opened her eyes, wincing at the sunlight. Her head throbbed, which usually meant she had consumed too much wine the night before. As her eyes focused, rusty metal bars came into view, which again wasn't that unusual.

What was unusual was that the cage she was in was suspended from a tree in the middle of a forest.

Events of the previous night came rushing back to her, and Syn lifted her hand to rub the bruise on her forehead. There was a small, painful lump and what felt like a bit of dried blood. She leaned over to peer out the side of the cage, which made the cage shift with her balance and swing from side-to-side. This attracted the attention of the beautiful witch who glanced up at her with disdain.

"Ah, I see our little thief has awakened."

Syn rubbed her forehead. "I wouldn't have caused you any harm."

"You mean other than taking everything we own?" the witch said. "And I hardly think you could cause us any harm. You're lucky you knocked yourself unconscious or we probably would have killed you instantly. Of course, now," she said, smelling the brew in the cauldron and adding another spice, "we'll get the pleasure of killing you slowly."

Syn sat down hard in the cage, causing it to swing back-and-forth. She was disgusted with herself. If she had a gold coin for every time she had been distracted by a pair of breasts or a nice backside she would, well, she would still be broke, as she gave everything away. But even so, it seemed to be her fatal flaw.

"So, I must know," the beautiful witch said, "you're obviously an accomplished thief as you had almost everything we own in your pockets." She cast her eyes upward and Syn noted they were a lovely shade of light green. "What happened?"

"I got distracted," Syn muttered, her self-disgust evident. She crossed her arms over her chest, which caused the cage to swing back-and-forth a little.

"And what distracted you?" the witch asked, returning to stirring her pot.

"If you must know," Syn said, her self-recrimination so pronounced she was bluntly honest, "I was enamored with your breasts."

This caught the witch's attention. She had been known to seduce the occasional handsome hunter then dispose of him when finished, but this intriguing little creature in the cage was a different matter. There was an unbalanced intensity about her that was strangely attractive, and the witch suddenly wondered what the woman might be like in her bedroll in the tent.

And this caught Syn's attention, for the expression on the witch's face, that hint of curiosity, was one with which she was well-familiar and willing to exploit. "Perhaps there's something I could do for you to make amends for my rude behavior," Syn said cautiously.

"Really?" the witch said with amusement, and Syn was doubly cautious. This was not some naïve farm girl she could take for a toss in the hay.

"Yes," Syn said, "I'm only good at two things. One is stealing."

"And the other?" the witch asked, entertained.

Syn allowed her dark green eyes to settle on the witch, then leisurely travel down the length of her body, lingering so that there was no doubt as to her intentions.

"I could better show you than tell you."

The witch stopped what she was doing, thoughtful. Then with a mere gesture she dropped the cage to the ground. It went hurtling downward, causing Syn's stomach to lurch in fear, then came to an abrupt halt where it briefly hovered, then settled gently on to the earth. Another gesture from the witch, and the hasp from the door was released and the gate swung open. Syn sat there for a moment, trying to calm her harsh breathing. This was a very powerful witch. She stood and stepped from the cage, brushing the dust from her clothing.

"Just so there's no misunderstanding," the witch said, "you're going to please me?"

"Yes," Syn said, "there's no misunderstanding." Her gaze went to the breasts once more.

"Then you'll please my sister first."

"What?" Syn said, startled. The comment was like a splash of cold water. She turned to the plain one, the one she had entirely forgotten about. The sister stood near the flaps of the tent.

"Of course," Syn stammered, far less enthusiastic about this plan.

The beautiful witch stepped toward her. "And if you're as talented as you think you are, then I'd better hear her scream."

"Of course," Syn stammered again. The plain sister held open a flap to the tent. Syn took a deep breath, walked to her, then ducked inside. The light was dim and Syn had a thought to get the matter over before her eyes adjusted to the faint light. The plain witch stared at her almost defiantly, then parted her robes and dropped them to the floor.

And all thoughts of hurry or fleeing left Syn. The woman was short, soft, rubenesque, even a little plump, but Syn so loved women. She moved to the witch and her hands slipped beneath the thin shift she wore, sliding upward to caress the breasts, then upward further to carry the shift over the woman's head. She went to her knees, which put her head on level with the woman's breasts and took each in her mouth hungrily while her hands slipped into the sheer undergarments. The warm skin smelled of mint and lavender. Syn's hands played and tortured while the woman put her hands on Syn's shoulders to brace herself and looked to the ceiling of the tent in disbelief. The hips began to undulate beneath the skilled hands between her legs and the flicking of the tongue on her nipples and she pressed Syn to her chest. Syn maneuvered her backward to the bedroll and lowered her to the ground, the hands and mouth barely pausing in their worship, and the woman responded because no woman needs to be beautiful, she merely needs to be thought beautiful, and that is what Syn's every move communicated.

Syn kissed her, deeply, then moved back down the body, her mouth and her hands trading places. The hands now playfully stroked the hardened nipples while the mouth trailed downward and settled between the legs. The witch cried out sharply at the probing tongue which then began a smooth rhythm that elicited near constant moaning. The sound made Syn smile, which almost caused her to lose rhythm, but she quickly regained it and brought the witch to a long and explosive climax. And in the end, the woman did in fact scream.

Syn rested for a moment, then pulled herself up onto the witch who now appeared far lovelier to her.

"And so, do you forgive me?" Syn asked, her dark green eyes laughing. The witch lightly slapped her on the face, then kissed her.

"Yes," she said, "I forgive you." She pushed Syn from her and rose from the bedroll, her movements languorous. "But you'll have to sate my sister." She pulled her robe on, languidly stretching. "She'll not be so easy on you."

Syn grinned and watched the witch leave. That had been incredibly fun. She leaned back in the bedroll and clasped her hands behind her head. Perhaps this would work out after all.

The flap to the tent opened once more and the other woman entered. Light green eyes assessed her and Syn felt far less comfortable all of a sudden.

"Why are you still dressed?" the witch demanded.

"I don't need to take off my clothes to please you," Syn said, even more uncomfortable.

"You're at least going to have to remove your pants to do what I want you to do," she said, making a deliberate gesture in Syn's direction.

Syn felt a very odd sensation in her pants and pulled out her waistband to peer down inside of them. "What is that?" she asked in disbelief.

"What does it look like?" the witch said, removing her robe. This was enough for Syn to tear her eyes away from her new appendage and stare at the loveliness before her. This witch was long-limbed, shapely, with full breasts with dark aureoles and a triangle of downy softness between her legs the same color as the hair on her head. Syn gazed at her for a long moment, but then her eyes returned to her new attachment. She reached down and touched the phallus-shaped object and it sprang erect.

"By the gods!" she said, startled, "I can feel it!"

The witch settled onto the bedroll beside her. "I'm not completely self-ish," she said, "I want you to take some pleasure as well."

She pulled Syn's shirt from over her head, and Syn was so fascinated by the appendage, for once she did not resist. The witch paused. The thief was quite a lovely human, not shapely but lithe and firm with breasts well-sized for her form. But what caught her eye was the series of crisscrossing scars down her back, thin and white against her tan skin. There was no redness to the markings at all, indicating they had healed long, long ago.

Syn caught her glance and looked away, her jaw clenched, but the witch didn't say anything, or at least anything about the scars. "Now your pants," the witch said determinedly, and Syn lifted her hips as the witch pulled her pants off. Another scar caught the witch's eye, this one on the woman's left thigh. This one appeared to be a burn, possibly left by a fireplace poker or a brand, and it, too, was white with age. She said nothing about the scar, but let her fingers trail over the surface which again made Syn's jaw clench, right up until the trailing fingers grasped her new phallus and she gasped out loud. It was no wonder kicking a man here was so effective.

"Do you know how to use one of these?" the witch casually inquired.

It was a very odd position to be in, Syn thought, the witch controlling her entire body by grasping something that wasn't even a part of her, at least in theory. "One of these? No, I've never had one of these. But I've used some accessories because a lot of women seem to like that." Syn was speaking very fast and her words were coming out all in a jumble.

"Well, let's see how you do," the witch said, positioning Syn on top of her, and then pulled her inside.

Syn had to grit her teeth. It was a wonder men did not climax immediately on penetration, although she did understand that to be a problem. "Just so we're clear on this, you're not going to leave this on me, are you?"

The witch laughed, enjoying the fullness between her legs. "That depends on whether or not you please me."

Syn moved her hips, marveling at the sensation, but then stopped again. "Just so I'm completely clear, if I please you, you're not going to leave it on me because I succeeded, are you?"

"If you don't get to work, you'll wear that for the rest of your life, which might be very short."

This was finally enough for Syn to release and she was perhaps even a little angry as she drove her hips into the witch. The sensation was intense, though, and Syn had to concentrate on not giving in to the pleasure. The beautiful witch, however, expressed no such reservation and Syn obtained great satisfaction that the woman's body responded wantonly as Syn drove her to orgasm twice. And it was finally driving her to a third that sent Syn over the edge and climaxing on top of her in as wanton a manner as the beautiful witch beneath her. Syn did not climax often so when she did, it was a fiery release.

The witch sighed with satisfaction as Syn collapsed on top of her. The witch ran her fingers on the whitened scars on the woman's back and side. She half-expected the thief to stiffen as she had before, but Syn's slow and steady breathing told the witch that the rakish thief was already asleep.

Syn awoke in the tent with no clear idea how long she had been asleep. It appeared to be dawn again, and now she wondered if she had slept almost an entire day. She recalled the previous day and glanced down, vastly relieved to see the appendage was gone. At least the witch had kept that part of her bargain.

She rose, dressed, then pushed her way through the flaps of the tent. The plain witch, who no longer seemed that plain to her but rather rosy and attractive, gave her an amused glance. The pale green eyes of her sister slid from the cauldron to their uninvited guest.

"Explain to me why I shouldn't go ahead and kill you," the witch said.

Any confidence Syn had gained from her performance in bed evaporated. "Well," she said uneasily, "I travel a great deal and it's possible I could be through this way again." The light green eyes looked at her skeptically, so she hurried on. "I could pay a tax, a toll if you will."

"Do you trade sexual favors for everything?" the witch asked with a penetrating stare.

Syn scuffed a boot while examining the ground. "Yes." She kicked at a rock. "Mostly just with women, although I find elven men handsome." She would not meet the witch's stare and had no idea why she was suddenly so confessional.

The witch stopped stirring. This really was a fascinating creature. Such an odd mixture of thievery and straightforwardness. It almost made her want to put the woman back in the cage. "I somehow doubt we'll see you again."

Syn's jaw clenched. That was a very true statement.

"But," the witch continued, "if you do pass this way, we'll make you pay the toll."

Syn nodded her understanding. She turned to the no-longer-plain witch and bowed. This was decidedly awkward. Normally she just snuck away after a sexual encounter, so standing here in broad daylight and bidding the two farewell was very odd.

"Go!" the green-eyed witch commanded, and Syn fairly sprinted into the forest. She could hear the women's laughter for quite some time.

CHAPTER 3

She was going to die, that was certain. It had been three days, or perhaps four, since her encounter with the witches. And although she had come away from the campsite with her life, she had not come away with any food. She had tried to eat a mushroom, which had made her vomit, then hallucinate, and she had tried to eat some berries, which just made her break out in a rash. She did find some nuts that weren't particularly tasty, but seemed edible, and that was probably the only reason why she was still alive.

When she smelled cooking again, she had two thoughts. One was that she had wandered in a gigantic circle and was now back with the witches, in which case it was her intention to sell herself into their sexual slavery for life as long as they would feed her. The second was that she was still hallucinating from the mushroom and that it was simply affecting a different sense. But the smell was irresistible and so she followed it. Perhaps it was the breeze or perhaps her hunger had heightened her sense of smell, but it was much further than she had expected. When at last she came to the edge of the forest, she was greeted with an idyllic scene.

A small cottage sat in front of a lake. It was impossible that someone lived out here in the wilderness, but there was a small, well-kept garden next to the house, a grindstone, and some chickens that pecked about in the grass. A tendril of smoke curled upward from the chimney and that seemed to be the source of that intoxicating aroma. Syn approached the cottage cautiously. She was not certain if it would be better if someone was home or not. If they weren't home, she could take what she needed and leave, but then she would still be wandering the wilderness hopelessly lost. If they were home, that could cause complications as well. She could be greeted warmly or with indifference, or she could be attacked on sight. She could hope it was some lonely widow, because really, right now, she would do almost anything for food.

She crouched down low and slowly pushed the door open. It made a little creak, but not much, and Syn waited to see if that caused a reaction. She did not hear any stirring or any footsteps, and she breathed a sigh of relief. She peeked around the corner and waited for her eyes to adjust. There didn't seem to be anyone home. She stood halfway upright and crept inside, her movement noiseless. Funny how she seemed to crash through the forest, vulnerable and exposed, yet the moment she was in a house her stealth took over and she disappeared into shadows.

A kettle was hanging from a spit over the fireplace and that appeared to be the source of the delicious smell. Syn started toward the pot, then stopped. As hungry as she was, her attention was drawn to the weapon that was lying on the table. It was a beautifully made bow and was likely worth a fortune. Perhaps her trek through the forest would not be a complete waste after all. The handiwork was so intricate it almost invited the hand to fondle it and she reached out.

"I wouldn't touch that if I were you," came the dry voice. Syn whirled, startled, toward the person who sat unmoving in the chair against the wall. "It's quite dangerous to the untrained." Stunning blue eyes flicked up and down her frame. "And you don't strike me as someone who's trained."

Syn froze. The woman was gorgeous with wheat colored hair and refined features, but that was not what struck Syn the most. Perhaps it was because

Syn operated on pure instinct, or perhaps it was her ability to read people, but one fact was overwhelmingly obvious to Syn: this was the most lethal individual she had ever seen. She hesitated a second longer, then gave up all pretense and darted for the door.

"That's a very bad idea," Raine murmured, getting to her feet.

The woman disappeared through the door and a thunderous roar shook the walls of the cottage. The terrified woman came sprinting back through the doorway, tripping and going to all fours yet still scrambling across the floor to where she hid behind Raine. Although the blue-eyed woman terrified her, what was outside was far worse.

"There's a dragon out there!" Syn said, her entire body shaking with fear.

"Yes," Raine said, "I know."

Something happened outside because there was brilliant flash of yellow light, and then another woman came strolling through the doorway. She was as striking as the first with silver hair and golden eyes, her chiseled cheekbones giving her an elegant and imposing air. She wore form-fitting, fiery red armor, and Syn could not help but note the armor was the same color as that dragon that had been outside.

"We seem to have a guest," Raine said mildly.

"I noticed," Weynild said, casting a malevolent stare in Syn's direction. Syn was used to being looked at with disapproval but this stare was withering. It actually caused her to sit down hard on the chair the blue-eyed woman had vacated. Raine hid a smile and moved to the table where she could sit across from the interloper and examine her. She was filthy and appeared to be starving. There were cuts and bruises on her everywhere, as if she had battled the forest and soundly lost. She was a thief, that much was obvious by her practiced entrance into the cottage, an entrance that would have gone undetected by anyone except Raine who possessed near-supernatural hearing. But there was something compelling about the roguish figure, as pathetic a condition as she was in at the present. And something sad in the way her eyes followed Weynild to the fireplace, settling on the kettle with inordinate longing.

"Are you hungry?" Raine asked.

"I'm famished," Syn admitted. "I haven't eaten in five days, other than some mushrooms and berries that nearly killed me, and some nuts that were so tasteless I wished for death."

Raine's gaze fell upon the woman's hands and arms: that would explain the rash. "Why don't you go wash up at the stream's edge and you can join us for dinner."

It was a most welcome invitation but Syn always distrusted acts of kindness. She got to her feet as those malevolent golden eyes slid around to her. "But isn't that dragon still out there?" Syn asked.

"I assure you," Raine said, "the dragon is no longer outside."

This comment made Syn very uneasy and she stared at the silver-haired woman a little harder. "Very well," she stammered, "I'll go wash up."

"Here," Raine said. She stood and walked to a nearby chest and removed a pair of pants and a shirt which she tossed to Syn. "Why don't you just," she looked at Syn's clothes, "burn those."

Syn took the clothes gratefully and walked out the door.

"She's probably already sprinting towards the forest," Weynild said.

"I think she's too hungry for that," Raine said.

And Syn was having the same debate with herself. She wanted to be running away, but she also wanted to be in that warm cottage eating dinner. The sun was going down, and she would happily sleep in that garden rather than in the forest. So, contrary to past practice and her very nature, she stripped, bathed, dressed in the comfortable clothing the woman had provided her, then walked back to the cottage.

Raine looked up at her entrance, then to Weynild. "It seems I won that wager."

"Hmm," Weynild said. "It's no matter. That wager rewarded me regardless of outcome."

Syn glanced from one to the other. She had been curious about their relationship, for it did not seem sisterly or maternal. Now it was evident it was neither. The heated intensity between the two was not subtle. Although strikingly different they were a striking pair and Syn found herself in the midst of her favorite entertainment, which was trying to imagine them naked, a pleasant picture right up until those golden eyes slid around to her as if reading her mind.

"Sit," the silver-haired woman said, and Syn complied as if she were a pet dog.

Raine provided her with a bowl of stew, then another, then another. Syn ate ravenously, and it was the best thing she had ever eaten. Her stomach felt like it was going to burst but it felt so good to be full again. She really wanted a fourth bowl but pushed away from the table.

"And so, what's your name?" Raine asked, placing a flagon of water in front of her.

"My name is Syn."

"Hmmph," Weynild said. That was appropriate.

"My name is Raine," the blue-eyed woman said, "and this is Weynild. Now how is it that you've found your way into the deepest wilderness in Arianthem?"

"I didn't find my way," Syn said, "I've been lost for days. My caravan was attacked by bandits and I fled into the forest to escape." Syn's expression darkened. "Then I came across two witches, and then, well...."

Syn drummed her fingers on the table.

"Two witches?" Weynild said with interest. "What did they look like?"

"One was very beautiful, with light green eyes, and one was very pleasantly plump, very soft and..." Syn again trailed off.

"The Raven sisters?" Weynild said, "Did you try and steal from them?"

"Yes," Syn said without a trace of prevarication. "And I almost succeeded, but then..."

Now Raine was interested, for there was obviously more to this story. Syn had not finished one of her last three sentences. "What happened?"

"I got distracted," Syn said, her expression clouding at the memory, "and I walked into a cast iron pot and knocked myself out cold. When I awoke I was swinging in a cage."

"And how did you get out of this cage?" Weynild said, querying the thief. "The Raven sisters don't let many trespassers live, let alone someone who tried to steal from them."

"I, um, I traded services," Syn said vaguely.

"What kind of services?" Raine asked, tilting her head.

"Sexual ones!" Syn exploded, "What do you think I did, till their garden?"

"Well, if you had said 'plow their fields' I might have said it was the same thing," Raine said, laughing. "The elder one is quite specific in her desires."

Weynild leaned over and glanced at Syn's pants. "She did remove it when you were through?"

"Yes," Syn said, rubbing her forehead, "thank the Divine. The things I do to get out of trouble."

"And how is that you get into so much trouble?" Raine asked.

Syn rolled her eyes. "I'm a thief," she said unrepentantly. "I steal things that belong to other people."

And now Raine had a very specific question for their guest. Syn had been forthcoming about her flaws and limitations, possessing a curious honesty for a thief. She had not shown any bravado, real or false.

"Are you a good thief?" Raine asked.

Syn was quiet for a moment. "I'm the best thief in all of Arianthem," she said simply, then frowned slightly. "Except when I'm distracted by breasts and things of that nature," she admitted

That did not surprise Raine. She had been greatly impressed by Syn's skilled entrance into the cottage. And the fact that she had gotten into the campsite of the Raven sisters was also impressive, for the elder had hearing almost as acute as Raine's.

"Are you a member of the Guild?" Weynild asked.

"No," Syn said dismissively. "I have no need of them."

"Isn't that dangerous?" Raine inquired.

"Of course. I've never met the man, but I've been told that Lagmann absolutely hates me."

Raine leaned back in her chair. Lagmann was the shadowy head of the Guild of Thieves. He could be a very powerful enemy.

"He's threatened several times to put a bounty on my head," Syn continued. "But two things keep the Guild at bay. First and foremost, they can't catch me. They think it's me. They've heard it's me. All sorts of rumors say it's me, but they can't prove it's me, and we never use the same fences, so they don't know what I've stolen. I always have a bounty on my head from the Empire, but that means nothing. But if the Guild were to put out a bounty, that would be bad."

"And how else do you keep the Guild at bay? You said there were two things." Raine said.

"Every once in a while, I do Lagmann a favor. Some job that no one else can do. He doesn't ask me personally; it always comes through a courier. But I know it's him, because the Guild always takes credit for it." Syn said with mild contempt. "I stole the Emperor's scepter right out from under his nose during his inauguration. No one from the Guild could do that."

"That was you?" Raine asked. That theft had been legendary and brought the Guild wide acclaim, or infamy anyway.

"I signed my name on his forehead while he was sleeping."

Comprehension dawned on Raine. The Imperial Guard had tried to keep the incident quiet, but the thief had written the word "sin" on the Emperor's forehead. Most assumed it was some sort of judgment, but clearly the rogue in front of her had simply left it as an autograph.

"I didn't spell it the same," Syn said, "I'm not completely stupid."

"Not completely," Weynild agreed drily.

"Well, Lagmann, from what I understand, wasn't too happy about that, either. But he got his scepter and the fame for his precious Guild."

"You like to live dangerously, don't you?" Raine said.

"Yes, yet another flaw of mine," Syn said.

"Is that what motivates you?" Weynild asked, suddenly intensely serious. Her golden eyes bored into Syn's and Syn, although she desperately wanted to, could not turn away. The golden eyes swept over her. "Because you obviously don't keep what you steal, so you're not driven by greed."

Syn's jaw clenched. How did you explain what motivated you when you weren't certain yourself? How did you explain that the numbness could only be chased away by terror and excitement, that you never felt so alive as when you were flirting with death? How did you explain that you were damaged beyond repair, flawed beyond redemption, and that the only moment that you were perfect was that second when everything hung in the balance and then you slipped away victorious?

Syn looked in the silver-haired woman's eyes and realized she didn't have to explain. There was an ancient wisdom there, a calculation, an assessment, but surprisingly little judgment. It was a startling moment for Syn, as if someone had finally peered into her, saw exactly who and what she was, yet offered up no verdict whatsoever.

"I have need of a thief," Weynild said.

"Really?" Syn said cautiously. These two were full of surprises, and that was saying something considering she suspected that one of them was a dragon.

"Yes," Weynild said smoothly, "and I don't wish to involve the Guild, so you seem to be perfect."

Syn looked from one to the other. "I don't know you that well, but I have a hard time believing there's anything you couldn't handle yourself."

Weynild gave a low, throaty chuckle and sensuality rippled outward from her like a wave. "I tend to attract a good deal of attention," she said, then glanced to Raine, "and this one kills everything that gets in her way."

Raine nodded. "'Tis true."

Syn shifted uncomfortably as Weynild continued. "And that's not what we need. We need stealth for this because it's not just one object but three. And once one is stolen, and then the second, the third will get much harder to acquire."

"What is it that you need stolen?" Syn asked, curious despite herself.

Weynild reached over and removed a bracelet from a small chest. She handed it to Syn. Syn took the object and turned it over in her hands. It was a silver circlet that had a single, milky stone set in it, but settings for three others

"This is a magical item," Weynild said. "Its purpose is not important. But it's useless without the other three stones."

Syn went to hand it to Raine, but Raine held up her hands. "I cannot touch it."

"Is it dangerous?" Syn asked quickly.

"No, no," Raine said, "but I disenchant magical items when I touch them."

"That's some trick," Syn said, finding that fact more interesting than the bracelet.

"Yes," Weynild said, bringing the conversation back. "It's likely that two of the possessors of the stones have no idea what they have, but the third most certainly does. And that one will be difficult. But it's crucial that all thefts are kept quiet. In fact, I would have you switch the stones so no one notices the thefts. The last person will know, but by then it will be too late."

"Right," Syn murmured. Her thoughts were racing. What a fantastic adventure. Three magical stones, three marks, everything done in complete secrecy. She knew the perfect person to counterfeit the stones, a talented jeweler who passed off fake jewelry to the nobility all the time, someone discreet who would ask no questions. She would prioritize the jobs according to difficulty, get the easiest done first...

"Aren't you even going to ask about payment?" Raine asked.

"What?" Syn said. "Oh, right, gold, whatever."

Weynild inwardly smiled. She had chosen well. Still, she would offer a reward.

"I will offer you something far more valuable than gold," Weynild said. "I'll offer you a favor."

"A favor?" Syn said.

"Yes," Weynild said, "Once this task is completed, I will be indebted to you. And you may call upon me when you're in need."

Such a statement would have been laughable from anyone else, but there was extraordinary gravity in the silver-haired woman's words.

"You—," Syn paused, "You're a dragon, aren't you?"

The golden eyes glowed. "Yes, I am. And I assure you that my young companion here, who is young to me but three hundred years older than you, is exceptional in her own way. And she will be at your service as well." Raine nodded formally in agreement.

Syn was excited, filled with more purpose and direction than at any other time in her life. "All right then," she said, just as formally, "you have a deal."

Syn was following a wolf who somehow knew exactly where to go. After a deep sleep in the cottage and a late rising, Syn had filled her stomach once more with eggs, bread, and cheese. Weynild was nowhere to be seen, but Raine had given her a pack full of dried meat, dried fruit, hardtack, and fresh water. She had confirmed their arrangements, verified that Syn knew where her first mark was, then pointed Syn in the direction of Havershire, the nearest village. And because it was clear that Syn would immediately get lost and never make it from the wilderness alive, Raine whistled and instructed the young wolf who responded to escort her from the forest. Syn would have thought the entire episode a hallucination caused by the mushrooms she had consumed except for the fact she was still following the wolf, a creature that the day before would have sent her fleeing in terror.

She reached Havershire far sooner than expected, but that is what happened when one walked in a straight line as opposed to endlessly in circles. She said goodbye to the wolf with some relief, then headed for the nearest tavern. Raine had also given her a bag of coin as she had left the witches' encampment with nothing on her other than her clothes. It was a testament to her newfound purpose and direction that she had left the small cottage without stealing a thing.

She was not completely redeemed however, and really, not even close, for the first thing that caught her eye upon entering the tavern was the buxom barmaid. And after retaining a room, flirting with the girl for several hours, plying her with just enough alcohol but not too much, she took the girl back to her bed and spent several more hours taking every last bit of her innocence.

CHAPTER 4

G renjad was a bustling city, not as large as the sprawling municipalities to the west, but much larger than the towns and villages that Syn had been frequenting of late. It was divided into three primary sections which themselves were subdivided further. The heart of the city was the merchant section which was filled with shops and the residences of the well-to-do tradespeople who ran them. To the south were the docks, a slum area inhabited by the poor and those who eked out a living working for the better-off. To the north were the homes of the nobility and the imperial keep.

Syn leaned against the wall as she contemplated the mansions on the hill, wondering what it would be like to live in one. Imperial soldiers could be seen mingling with private guards, creating a safe haven for the wealthy. Syn snorted; that was a false sense of security if she had ever seen one. She returned her attention to the merchant square. There were a lot of soldiers and guards down here as well. That was probably why so many of the nobility were prancing about in their finery. Although she was only here to see the jeweler, she was very tempted to take down a few marks.

"Well, well, well," Fafner said.

Syn turned toward the voice and winced. She knew that the Guild had a strong presence in the city, she had just hoped to avoid them since she wasn't planning on being in Grenjad that long. That possibility disappeared as she had just been spotted by one of the highest-ranking Guild members in the region. Perhaps it had not been wise to lounge about so leisurely in the open.

"Fafner, my old friend," Syn said in a tone that suggested they were not friends. The tone, however, did not imply that they were enemies.

"And what might you be doing in Grenjad?" Fafner asked, "Business or pleasure?"

"Is there a difference," Syn replied, "when you do what you love?"

Fafner's tone had been lightly mocking, but he grew serious. "You should be careful, girl. Lagmann's grace with you will only extend so far."

"And is Lagmann already tired of playing with the Emperor's scepter?" As she said this, she made a very crude gesture of sliding her curled hand up and down an imaginary staff.

Fafner had to laugh. Syn was incorrigible and it was hard not to like her. It was just that she was so damn stubborn and reckless.

"Why is it you won't join the Guild?" Fafner said, starting the same conversation they had already had numerous times.

Syn's eyes flicked to the crowd in the square. "Why? So, I can take orders and steal petty items for money? You know I don't take instruction well."

"You could be Lagmann's right hand, take only big jobs. Nothing small or petty."

Syn was silent for a long moment, then simply repeated, "You know I don't like to take orders."

Fafner sighed. It was always the same. Sooner or later, Lagmann was going to have this one's head.

"How do you restrain yourself?" Syn mused, "With so many cattle and sheep about?"

Fafner knew she was talking about the wealth that was on prominent display in the square. The nobility were absolutely foolish in their exhibition. But part of the reason for their level of comfort was that, unbeknownst to them, the Guild had placed the merchant square off limits. It was important to set boundaries, to allow certain areas to thrive. And the merchants gladly paid a small percentage of their profits to keep the square clean.

"Don't be foolish, girl," Fafner warned.

Syn dismissed him with a wave. "I'm here to see a jeweler, nothing more. It's on a separate, private matter, and I'll be gone as soon as he's finished."

"Good," Fafner said. But that did not stop him from leaning against the wall next to Syn as she continued to peruse the crowd.

There were a few elves in the throng, and Syn picked out a dwarf. But for the most part, it was men and women. They were all dressed stylishly, even the tradespeople. It made Syn very conscious of her simple clothing, and she was glad she was leaning against the wall out of the center of things.

One woman in particular caught Syn's eye. She was accompanied by four personal guards and was greeted with tremendous respect. She returned the greetings with polite reserve. Her dress bore the mark of high nobility, possibly even some minor royalty as it was simple but extremely elegant, eschewing ostentation for true style. It was a deep green bordered with gold thread, and it set off a pair of stunning blue-green eyes. She wore an unassuming gold chain around her neck which matched gold earrings, but they were well-made to Syn's practiced eye. Her skin was the color of cream and just the hint of a swell of breasts could be seen above the cut of the gown. She twirled, the lovely dress swaying gracefully, and began examining some items on the table. Syn was disappointed as she could no longer see her breasts, but her disappointment was assuaged by the fact she now had a wonderful view of her backside and the curves set off so enticingly by that alluring dress. Syn was normally subtle in her observation, but right now she was openly staring.

Fafner followed her gaze and chuckled out loud. He was well aware of Syn's penchant for womanizing.

"That one is too expensive for you in oh-so-many ways."

Syn's cheeks grew hot and she turned to him. "Shut up," she said, embarrassed that she had been so obvious.

Fafner continued to chuckle. "The Lady Jorden is well-connected within the Empire and has even been known to hire the Guild on occasion."

"Really," Syn said, "someone like that would involve themselves with the Guild?"

"Ah," Fafner replied, "the rich rarely do it for money. With them it's generally about political advantage or revenge."

Syn would not ask because she knew Fafner would not tell, and she returned to her inspection of the woman. What would it be like to be born into such wealth and privilege? And what would it be like to have such softness in the bed next to her? Syn again became very conscious of her rough clothing, of her rough image, her lanky frame, the scars on her back. She knew that she was not beautiful, not like the "Lady Jorden." She might be mildly attractive to some hayseed farm girl, but not to this noblewoman.

Her thoughts made her angry and she pushed away from the wall. "Hopefully the jeweler will have what I need, and I'll be gone tomorrow," she said to Fafner. "I'll be down on the docks until then."

"Keep your hands clean," Fafner directed her retreating back, and she simply waved acquiescence.

The merchant watched the Lady Jorden with anticipation. She had been holding that mirror for a lengthy spell, and he was certain she was going to make a purchase. But what he didn't know was that she was holding it at a very specific angle, one that caught a second reflection from a table mirror that was also on display. And as Syn stood leaning against the wall, a parade of emotions crossing her face including longing, desire, shame, and anger, the Lady Jorden had been watching her the entire time.

Vestein's head swiveled up as a customer came through the door. He smiled. This was not a customer. In fact, this was nothing but trouble. But Syn had once helped him when he had been hit hard by thieves. He had complained to the Guild and they had done nothing, but Syn had overheard and, bold as you please, had gone and stolen everything right back. He tried to pay her for it, but she refused, saying it had all been in fun.

Syn did not ask him to fence things, for that was not his talent or his desire. The majority of Vestein's business was completely legitimate and Syn would not jeopardize that. However, Vestein had one amazing talent that Syn often made use of, which was his ability to counterfeit almost any item shown to him. There were several wealthy patrons throughout Arianthem that wore fake goods about their necks, unaware that the originals had ever been stolen. It was sometimes easier to replace things than to outright steal them, especially if the item was particularly rare or valuable.

Syn waited while Vestein finished with his customer, then he waved her to follow him into the back of the shop. She pulled a wrinkled piece of parchment from her pocket and showed it to him.

"I need three of these," Syn said, "they're shaped like this, and this is very close to the color."

Vestein examined the drawing. Syn made it easy on him because she was a good artist. She had even taken care to mix some chalk and a few dyes to get the color right.

"It looks very similar to an opal," Vestein commented, "with that milky color."

"Yes, exactly. And it's enchanted, so it glows a little."

"Ah," Vestein said with some excitement. That part would be challenging. He had a few ideas, including a sample of some glowing moss that had been brought to him by some adventurer who found it deep in a cave. Perhaps he could use some of the spores from that plant.

"Can you do it?" Syn asked.

"Of course," Vestein said, "it'll take me a few days, but I already have some starter stones that will get me going quickly."

"Good," Syn said, relieved. She had been afraid he might not be able to recreate the items. "I can pay you any way you like, gold, jewelry, precious stones."

"No," Vestein insisted, "I could make a thousand of these for you and it wouldn't pay for what you did for me and my family." And that was true, for not only had Vestein lost his personal supply in the theft, he had lost many of his client's pieces as well, which would have ruined him. Syn had retrieved every last piece, and even a few extra that she had simply shrugged and told him to keep.

Syn patted him on the shoulder. "Thanks, friend. I'll check back in a few days."

The docks were bustling with activity, and because she was now amongst her people, it meant that all the taverns would be humming even though it was early in the day. She thought to head to the Fish Head Inn, a rough and tumble sort of place that at least was clean. She could probably get a room there fairly cheap because the waitresses all loved her. And a few days of drinking and debauchery would help pass the time and keep her out of trouble, or at least out of the kind of trouble that involved stealing things.

"Ah, there you are."

Syn turned to see Fafner coming up the street toward her. He was accompanied by two other rough-looking fellows. She held up her hands.

"Whatever it was, I didn't take it," she said.

"A little sensitive, are we?" Fafner said, and Syn relaxed. His tone was not accusatory. In fact, judging by his demeanor, he looked like he wanted something. He motioned to the alley, indicating his two companions were to stay at the entryway, and Syn followed him in. Fafner got right to the point.

"I have a job for you."

Syn crossed her arms and leaned against the wall. "Didn't we already have this conversation?"

"It's from Lagmann."

Syn's expression sobered as Fafner continued. "He knows you're in town and he has something that's very suitable for your particular talents."

"I'm listening," Syn said.

"There's a mansion up on the hill, and a locket on the third floor of this mansion, a locket that a particular client wants very badly."

"Aren't you shitting in your own bed?" Syn asked sarcastically. "I didn't think the Guild did business in Grenjad."

"Why do you think we're asking you?" Fafner said.

"Oh," Syn said, "I see. Get an outsider to do your dirty work. Couldn't you get it done and then deny all knowledge? As long as the thief doesn't get caught, they won't know who it is."

"And that's the other reason why Lagmann wants you. This mansion is heavily guarded. The outer walls are covered by imperial soldiers, and the inner courtyard is patrolled by private guardsmen. It's probably one of the most secure locations in all Arianthem."

"Probably not as secure as the Imperial Palace," Syn commented.

"Exactly," Fafner said, "which is why Lagmann is asking this of you. And he wants it done tonight."

"He doesn't ask for much, does he?" Syn said, even more sarcastic.

"Look," Fafner said, "this is a simple job for you. Do it, and you'll buy six more months of grace with the Guild. Refuse, and you may not make it out of town."

"Fine, fine," Syn said, "I'm glad you caught me before I started drinking. Just give me the details."

Fafner took out the piece of parchment that had been passed to him. "Everything is here. I'll tell Lagmann you agreed."

CHAPTER 5

Syn was crouched in the shadow of the large oak tree in the center of the inner courtyard. She had already made it past the Imperial Guard with little effort. The armor they wore clanked so loudly she could tell exactly where they were without even looking. One small distraction, and she had slipped in the gate right behind them. And now she was analyzing the layout with a critical eye, thinking she would have fired the gardener for not trimming this tree because the branch was close enough to the second story ledge she could leap from one to the other, saving her from having to run across the open expanse stretching between her and the mansion. There were many private guards milling about, but none of them were looking up, and that was where she was going to be.

She scaled the tree and inched along the limb, careful not to rustle any leaves or dislodge any branches. The jump from the tree to the wall would be something of a feat, but she waited for that fraction of a second where all the guards were turned in a fortuitous direction and leaped. She landed lightly on the ledge with only a little waver of imbalance that she corrected, then began to move stealthily down the overhang. She was built perfectly for this kind of work, tall enough to reach things many could not, slender enough to walk down ledges from which many would fall, and strong and agile enough to maintain her balance in precarious positions. It was much easier to enter a residence from the second or third floor than to enter it from the bottom level and try to work one's way up once inside.

Syn reached up, anchoring her fingers on the ledge above her, then pulled herself silently upward so that she was now on the third floor. The instructions had been quite specific and the window to the room that she wanted was four down. She moved down the ledge, ducking beneath each window that she passed, until she came to one that she wanted. She jimmied the latch on the wooden shutters, then slowly pushed them inward, praying that they did not creak. They were solid and well-made, as she would expect from a household of this manner, and they did not make a sound.

Syn crawled through the window and dropped lightly to the floor. She waited for a moment, orienting herself. There was a bed to her left, and a chest of drawers to her right. Next to the wall near her was a table with a decorative plate propped up in display. It was a fairly large room and the part between the bed and chest was in deep shadow, illuminated only slightly by a dimly glowing oil lamp. The shadowed area bothered Syn; she did not like to move until she was certain she was alone, so she crouched there for a considerable duration. But there was nothing else in the room, so she stood and stretched from her cramped position. The chest likely held the locket, so she would have to pick that lock. She took the lock-picking tools from her pocket, and with startling swiftness, popped the clasp open as if she had the key.

"You are good," the voice said from the shadows. Syn whirled, startled, and nearly knocked the decorative plate from its stand. She juggled the plate as a disembodied hand reached from the shadows and lengthened the wick on the oil lamp, illuminating the room with soft light. Syn continued to juggle with the plate, keeping it from falling but not from making a lot of noise in the process.

"And then you make a liar out of me," the Lady Jorden said. There was a commotion at the door and several guards charged in.

"M'lady," said the first, his sword drawn, "we heard a noise—"

"I'm fine," Jorden said smoothly, her eyes never leaving Syn. "I'm simply entertaining a guest."

The guard looked from the mistress of the house to Syn, then back again. "A guest," he said, eying Syn skeptically, "of course." He bowed to Jorden. "We'll take our leave, then."

"Captain?" Jorden said, stopping the man halfway to the door. "Double the guards throughout the house and the yard below."

The captain bowed. "Of course, m'lady." He gave Syn one last threatening scowl and left the room.

Syn stood frozen. She was astonished to see the noblewoman in the room with her, and even more astonished that she sat there calmly, unperturbed, almost as if she had been expecting her. There was something unnerving about her demeanor, so much so that Syn took a step backward when the woman got to her feet. But Jorden merely walked past her to the window to glance into the courtyard below.

"Interesting," she said. "Even though the guards knew you were coming, they couldn't catch you."

Syn found her voice, although her tone was uncertain. "How could they know I was coming?"

Jorden closed the shutters and fastened the latch, an action that somehow was even more unnerving than her cool composure. She turned to Syn.

"Who do you think contracted with the Guild for your services?"

Syn still did not understand. "You're the client? But why would you hire me to break into your own home?"

The blue-green eyes captured Syn and held her hostage while the full lips twitched in amusement. "You're a little slow, aren't you?" Jorden said softly. She slid her hands about Syn's waist and pulled her to her, kissing her. The softness of her lips was a perfect contrast to the hardness of the kiss, but Syn was so stunned she barely returned it. Jorden pulled back from her, then reached around her neck and undid the tie that held her hair. The shoulder length locks fell about her face, transforming her features in a manner in which Jorden clearly approved.

"That's better," she said.

It finally dawned on Syn what was happening, and she went to kiss Jorden, but the woman stopped her.

"No," she said softly but firmly. She reached out and undid the buttons down the front of Syn's shirt, and Syn reached out to do the same to her gown.

"No," she said again, even more firmly as if Syn were some disobedient child. Syn was confused and even a little angry at the game the woman was playing with her. Jorden saw the beginnings of rebellion and cut it short.

"Just so there's no misunderstanding here," she said, leaning close to whisper in Syn's ear, "you've been caught breaking into the manor of one of the most powerful women in all of Arianthem. I could turn you over to my guards, I could turn you over to the empire, or I could turn you over to the Guild."

This last threat caused Syn to pale slightly, and Jorden continued.

"So, you're going to let me do exactly as I will." Jorden's hands slipped inside Syn's shirt, settling upon her waist. "Come," she said with a gentle command.

And Syn found herself maneuvered backward into the bed just as she had done to so many women. Jorden settled next to her, propping herself up on one elbow. With her other hand, she spread Syn's shirt apart, her gaze settling on the firm breasts with pleasure. Syn watched her in a daze, still numb from what was happening. Her breasts were not numb, however, as Jorden took one in her hand, cupping then caressing it, and it sprang to life beneath her touch.

Syn reached up to touch her, and Jorden caught the hand. "I'll not tell you again," she said, and it was difficult to tell how much was admonishment and how much was threat. She placed Syn's hand at her side and Syn felt exposed beneath her gaze. Those blue-green eyes assessed her body, but kept returning to her face, enjoying the reaction and parade of emotions as much as the feel of the flesh beneath her fingers. The fingers traveled lower, trailing across the tense stomach, then undoing the tie of her pants. Jorden loosened them, then slipped her hand into the waistband and pressed her fingers to the warmth below.

Syn was desperately trying to control her reaction, but she could not stifle the gasp this elicited, which clearly gave Jorden enormous pleasure. Jorden stroked the softness very purposefully, watching for Syn's response. Syn tried to suppress it, tried to maintain a semblance of control, but her hips moved a little and she could feel the wetness come. That in itself was unusual, for it generally took Syn a very long time for her body to respond to pleasure, yet this woman was bringing it forth with hardly a touch. Syn felt very vulnerable beneath her gaze, and somehow the fact that Syn was almost fully dressed, with only her shirt parted and Jorden's hand in her pants, heightened that vulnerability more so than had she been fully naked. And the blue-green eyes locked onto hers made the situation somehow more intimate than had the Lady Jorden's head been buried between her legs.

Jorden watched the mass of confused emotions she was bringing forth, and it excited her. Still, she was in perfect control as the hand explored.

"What is this from?" Jorden asked as Syn stiffened. The hand had found the scar on her thigh and now traced its long, linear outline. Syn's jaw clenched and it appeared at first, she would not answer, but Jorden's gaze did not brook disobedience. She leaned down closer to Syn.

"That's from my first theft," Syn said quietly. "I got caught and that was my punishment."

The blue-green eyes examined her as the hand caressed the scar. "And what did you steal?"

"I was starving, and I stole a loaf of bread."

The hand caressed the scar, then trailed back to between her legs, returning to its methodical stroking. Syn fought to keep her hips from rising to meet the fingers but was only partially successful. She had the impression that Jorden was enjoying her attempted resistance as much as her response. The fingers continued their exploration of the area, this time finding the thin scars that began on her hip and crisscrossed upward along her side until they crossed her back.

"And what are these from?" Jorden asked.

Syn twisted away. "Punishment from another failed theft," she said dismissively.

Jorden's exploration stopped and she reached up and took Syn's chin in her hand, turning her head and forcing Syn to look at her. The blue-green eyes looked at her penetratingly. "You're lying to me." Her hand slipped down inside the shirt to the scars, fingering them. "Now what are these from?"

Syn was growing angry. This woman was exerting a perverse control over her and she was incapable of stopping her. If she wanted the truth, she would give it to her.

"My parents were killed by Hyr'rok'kin when I was eight years old. A few months later, a prostitute took me in. And a few years after that, she took me to her bed."

Contrary to Syn's expectations, Jorden was less shocked than intrigued, and even perhaps a little aroused by the admission. "And how old were you?" she murmured.

"Young," Syn said, her jaw clenching, "very young."

"Hmm," Jorden said, wanting to know the entire story. Her fingers returned to the scars. "And so, she punished you?"

Syn's jaw worked furiously. "No," she said, biting off the word, "she beat me because it brought her sexual pleasure."

Jorden's hand stopped and she stared down at Syn. She had a look of incredible intensity on her face. "I won't hurt you," Jorden murmured.

The hand slipped back between her legs and Syn was very frightened of the woman on top of her. Because although her words said she would not hurt her, her eyes said that she would dominate her, possess her, and utterly own her. And the fingers stroked, then slipped inside her as Jorden leaned down and kissed her, her tongue probing as skillfully as her fingers. She seemed greatly pleased at the confession she had elicited and this time the hand was unrelenting. She stroked and caressed and now the hips would not stay in control but rather moved beneath the taskmaster with abandon. And Syn, who never made a noise during sex, was driven to near frenzy and at last cried out with a release she had rarely known.

Syn lay on her back staring up at the ceiling, conscious of the blue-green eyes that were coolly assessing her. Jorden rolled her onto her side so that Syn was facing away from her, then settled in behind, pressing against her and throwing an arm possessively about her waist. Syn's thoughts were a confused mass and she felt numb. Usually it was her role to bring a woman to pleasure then quickly fall asleep, so she was well aware of Jorden's deepened breathing behind her as she lay staring into darkness.

After an hour or so, Syn at last had enough sense to slip the arm from her waist and rise silently from the bed. She retied the rope about her pants and buttoned her shirt with fingers that still felt numb. Any thought of a locket or a job had long since slipped away. She carefully undid the latch to the shutters, and noiselessly pulled them open. The voice from the bed caused her to pause.

"Though I've doubled the guard downstairs," Jorden said, "I have no doubt you'll elude them."

Syn turned to her, saying nothing.

"But I tell you this," Jorden said, her blue-green eyes penetrating once more. "If you leave Grenjad or attempt to flee in any way, I will have you hunted down like a dog. You, your friends, anyone who is even slightly dear to you, they will all suffer."

Syn looked at her, then pulled herself out onto the ledge.

Jorden watched the figure disappear and was actually glad that she had left. She had wanted to maintain complete control with Syn but had been so close to losing it. Now her hand slipped between her own legs and she began providing herself the pent-up release that gorgeous, complicated little thief had inspired. And before Syn had even made it out the front gate, Jorden had brought herself to climax, her eyes unfocused and her thoughts on those beautiful scars.

CHAPTER 6

S yn leaned against the wall in a very dark reverie. She had returned to the inn, but sleep had been elusive. She had wandered the docks, but not even the card games could hold her attention. Finally, she had returned to the merchant square, leaning insolently against the wall and thinking about fleecing the lot of them.

Despite the Lady Jorden's very credible threats, Syn was leaving the minute Vestein was finished with her stones. There was no doubt that woman would lose interest with someone of her ilk almost immediately. The whole night seemed a shadowy dream, a passionate, frightening, intense dream. Apparently, the nobility could be as perverse as the common folk.

Syn's gaze grew distant and although still watching the throng of merchants, she was no longer seeing them. She had to admit, though, part of the reason she was standing here was the possibility of seeing Jorden again. The thought sent a chill through her, one that was commandingly counterbalanced by the thrill it also generated, not to mention the stab of desire that twisted in her torso. Syn grew angry. She had no idea how that woman had manipulated her into revealing so much of herself, things she had never told anyone. Nor did she have any idea why she was so submissive to Jorden. It was not the fact that she was nobility; Syn viewed most nobles with contempt. It wasn't her wealth because wealth did not impress Syn. Jorden wasn't particularly physically imposing, although she had been surprisingly strong for a noblewoman.

No, the Lady Jorden seemed to have some sort of power over her that defied explanation. And when she had told Syn that she would not hurt her but looked at her as if she owned her, Syn had almost climaxed on the spot. By the gods, had that woman identified some deep weakness in her? This thought made Syn even angrier and made her want to go back to the Inn and drive one of the bar maids to ecstasy, but then her anger increased even more because she thought perhaps that was why she did such things in the first place.

Syn rubbed her eyes. Her head hurt. She returned her attention to the square, aware that the guards were taking a particular interest in her. She wondered if it was because they saw her as a threat but thought it more likely that Jorden had handed down an edict as promised. The guards had not watched her that way yesterday, and she had been just as much a thief then.

Fafner was approaching and she looked to him with a combination of disgust and disdain. Knowingly or unknowingly, he had set her up, and that fucker Lagmann was probably laughing even now. Fafner's expression told her that he knew, at least in part, that the job had not been what it seemed.

"I have something else for you," Fafner said uncomfortably. He held a piece of parchment, much like he had the day before. Syn snatched the paper from his hand, reading it quickly. It was the same directions as the previous day, the only difference being that the "client" said she could enter by the back gate. She stared hard at Fafner.

"I thought you were a thief, Fafner, not a pimp."

Fafner struggled with his own demons, for those had been exactly his thoughts. But he liked Syn and she was in deep on this one.

"Look," he said, "Lagmann is already very nearly your enemy; you don't want the Lady Jorden in that category as well. She's immensely powerful and can do things to you that even the Guild cannot."

"Yes," Syn said, "I think I experienced some of those things last night, thank you very much."

"Syn..." Fafner began.

"Shut up," Syn said. She waved her hand, "and just go. Leave me alone."

Fafner departed and Syn leaned back against the wall, her thoughts returning to the very dark place they were beginning to call home.

Syn wrestled with herself all day long, but when the sun went down, she found her legs trudging up the hill once more. She told herself it was because Vestein was not yet finished and she had to maintain peace while she was in town, but she was not so dishonest to maintain that was the entire reason. She would not, however, enter the back gate like some servant.

Jorden looked up from her book as Syn crawled through the window. "I told you that you needn't sneak in again."

"Yes," Syn said, standing upright and brushing her hands. "I'll not come through the back gate."

"Would you rather come through the front?" Jorden asked.

"I'd rather not come at all," Syn replied.

"Don't be rude," Jorden chastised with a trace of menace.

Syn snorted and Jorden stood. Apparently, her little thief was feeling rebellious once more. She moved to her and although Syn was tall, they stood eye-to-eye. She reached around and loosened her hair so that it fell about her face once more.

"I like your hair down," Jorden said, and Syn felt some small sense of satisfaction because that is why she had put it up. Jorden's gaze swept her frame. "Now take off your clothes."

"What?" Syn said, startled.

"Yesterday you were slow, today you're deaf? Here, let me help you."

Jorden grabbed the lapels of her shirt and gave them a short, sharp yank, causing the buttons to go flying. It wasn't so much a violent move as one extremely effective, and the shirt was on the floor at Syn's feet.

"I know that's probably the only shirt you own," Jorden said mockingly, "but I'll buy you another one."

Syn's cheeks flushed red with anger, but before she could respond, Jorden had pushed her back onto the bed, removed one light boot, then the other, then with one smooth yank, pulled her pants off in another singularly effective maneuver. Syn was reminded of how many times she had skillfully undressed women and had to admit that Jorden's technique put her to shame.

Jorden stared down at her with considerable pleasure. She had not had the opportunity to examine the woman's full body the night before, and now she did so leisurely. It was lean, not the gauntness of hard, manual labor, but not the softness of a pampered life, either. Her attention was drawn magnetically to the scar on the thigh, then to the thin white lines that curled around the hip and up the side.

"I should tie you up," Jorden said, thinking aloud, then regretted her frankness for Syn sat bolt upright and began to scramble from the bed. Jorden caught her, using her weight to keep Syn in place. "Shh," she said, kissing her, correctly guessing that Syn had been restrained before, probably during the acquisition of the scars on her back. She pressed her gently into the bed. "I won't do that to you," she said, then half to herself, "at least not yet."

Syn wanted to struggle but found herself once again submitting to this woman's strange combination of dominance, protectiveness, and possession. It was almost maternal, but sexually charged, and Syn had a sudden, prescient curiosity: she knew what had caused her damage, why she was the way she was, but now she wondered what drove the Lady Jorden to such acts.

She did not have long to ponder such thoughts because Jorden had already fully taken command. Her lips went to the scars she had merely caressed the night before, and her tongue traced the outline of each thin mark, following the path up her side. The feeling was exquisite to Syn, the area already highly sensitive and the flicking of the tongue making it even more so. The lips traveled sideways to the breasts where the mouth settled onto the mound and the tongue began to play with the nipple, teasing and torturing. Jorden's hand moved downward and Syn thought it would settle between her legs but instead it began to caress the scar, a torture in its own way because it was close to what throbbed and desired attention.

Then the lips moved downward, but they did not settle on the throbbing but rather toyed with the scar on her thigh, licking, kissing, then feathering the kiss sideways down the length which finally put the mouth between the legs, causing Syn to come up out of the bed once more. Jorden laughed, pushing Syn back down with one hand while thrusting the fingers of the other up inside her. And the mouth continued its business, the lips moving with gentle pressure and the tongue gently licking and darting about until Syn climaxed at the demand and command of that rapacious mouth. She was again shocked at how effortlessly this woman brought her to pleasure when most women could not do it at all.

Jorden pulled her body up onto Syn so she could gaze in her eyes. Her own blue-green were filled with triumph. And Syn heard herself speak words that had been directed at her so many times.

"Why is it you won't allow me to please you?"

"Didn't I look like I was enjoying that?" Jorden replied.

The words angered Syn, mocked her, for it was a version of her standard response. She sought to get up, but Jorden held her down, and when she began struggling, Jorden held her tighter. She was again astonished at Jorden's strength, and the fact that the woman appeared to enjoy the struggle made her even angrier. But Jorden's tolerance for Syn's disobedience was limited.

"Stop it," she commanded, and Syn stopped, which then made her even angrier and she started struggling again.

"I won't tell you again," Jorden said, "if you don't stop struggling, I'll call my guards in here and have you tied spread-eagle to this bed."

This threat was enough to quiet Syn, probably because it so obviously aroused Jorden it was possible she might carry it out regardless.

"That's better," Jorden said. She would not tell this rakish little thief she had every intention of putting her on her knees and holding her head in her hands while that smart little mouth of hers drove her to ecstasy. She would not tell her that the minute Syn crawled out the window Jorden would bring herself to climax to release the pressure that threatened to overwhelm her even now. No, she would break her first, bring out the submission she knew ran deep beneath her surface, then, and only then, would she allow this one's formidable skill in bed to touch her.

But Syn knew none of that and saw Jorden's reticence through the prism of her own life and her own motivations. Clearly the Lady Jorden did not think she was capable of pleasing her.

Syn was again leaning against the wall in her favorite spot in the market square. She was feeling quite surly at the moment, although for once she blended in with the rest of the crowd and that was part of what was making her surly. She was clothed very nicely because the Lady Jorden had insisted on dressing her before she left. It was both erotic and humiliating to be dressed by the woman, who rotated her to-and-fro as she examined her from every angle, at last satisfied with her appearance.

Even worse was the fact that the clothing was fantastic. It fit her perfectly, was soft and comfortable, and was simple in design but stylish. The colors were muted, tans and browns, which again fit her perfectly. She had received several admiring glances from people who had looked right through her the day before.

And now, it seemed, the Lady Jorden could not help but come down from her throne room and look upon her pet creation, for Jorden walked into the square accompanied by her usual entourage of guards and servants, holding court amongst the commoners. She returned greetings with her polite, icy, reserve, but the blue-green eyes sought Syn out and were filled with fire as she languorously examined her domesticated captive. Jorden did not stay long, but Syn was very aware of the scrutiny of the guards when she departed. The bars of her cage weren't visible, but they were there, nonetheless.

Syn saw Vestein's son wave to her from across the square. That meant that the stones were finished. She pushed away from the wall and started through the square, passing Fafner on her way. He looked at her in surprise.

"That's a nice shirt," he said, truly intending the compliment.

"Shut up," Syn said.

The Lady Jorden stood looking out into her courtyard. The chief of her security forces was behind her, as well as her closest personal servant, Helga. They both stood silently, unwilling to draw the attention of their mistress, for her anger was visceral.

"And you're certain she's gone?" Jorden said.

"Yes m'lady," the captain said. "We've searched the city high and low. She's nowhere to be found."

Jorden nodded, furious but not surprised. She was about to have Syn imprisoned on some imaginary charges, having already arranged for an extended house arrest. She had sensed the thief was about to bolt, and apparently had missed her by hours.

"I don't think I need to express to you how disappointed I am in you and your men," Jorden said.

The captain swallowed hard. When the Lady was this calm it usually meant she was seething, which would not bode well for any of them. They had been tasked to watch a single individual and had failed. There was nothing he could say, so he said nothing.

"You will convey my disappointment to General Othin, as well," Jorden said, turning to the captain. "He and his imperial troops did no better. You will tell him that this thief stole my diamond necklace and that I wish a bounty on her head."

The captain nodded.

"And finally," Jorden said, returning to the window, "you will convey my deep displeasure to Fafner as, surprisingly, his people also failed me. And you will strongly suggest I would look with favor if Lagmann placed a private bounty on the thief's head."

The captain again nodded. "Of course, m'lady. Is there anything else?"

Jorden was thoughtful for a long moment. As angry as she was, she had to admit she was a little impressed. That woman had outsmarted her private guards, the imperial soldiers, and the Guild itself, all of which had been on constant surveillance. Her admiration, however, would not stop her from hunting Syn down and making her pay.

"Yes," she said smoothly, "get that jeweler in here."

It was pouring down rain and the barn looked inviting. The animals were all safe inside and the farmer and his wife were cozy in their cottage. It was unlikely they would come out the rest of the evening. Syn crouched and moved silently across the open field, wrinkling her nose at the smell of the pigs. She would sleep on the far side of the barn, away from the smell. She undid the wooden bar on the barn door and entered, leaving the door slightly ajar in case she had to make a quick escape.

She climbed up into the loft and found a nice pile of hay, the fresh smell blocking out the odor of the pig manure. The barn was well-constructed and had few leaks, none near her. She pressed the hay down flat to make something of a nest, then settled into the soft pile. There was a slight chill from the window up above her head, but there was little wind and the rain was coming almost straight down. It was actually pleasant, and Syn put her hands behind her head.

She had run from Grenjad. Vestein's stones had been perfect and the minute they were in her pocket, she ducked the guards that were following her, dove into the water off the docks, and swam for her life. She was a good swimmer, one of her few skills beyond stealing things. Once on the path on the other side of the inlet, she had swiped a necklace from the first traveler she passed, which she then used to secure passage on a wagon heading away from the city. In the first village, she had seen an attractive widow who rebuffed her attentions, so she then stole everything of value from her home that evening. In the second village, she found a seamstress who was willing to make her new clothing as well as share her bed, and Syn gave her everything she had stolen from the widow, pretty much setting her up for the rest of her life. In the third village, she found a drunken, angry bard with huge breasts that spilled out over her top as she spilled her drink on Syn, and the two then had angry sex so the bard could make up for the accident that Syn had orchestrated.

So, it was somewhat of a relief to lie in the hay in the barn and listen to the gentle rain which had slowed from its torrent. She had been acting even more reckless than usual, and she would have to calm down because she was getting close to her first mark with the stones. The irresponsible fuck-and-steal fest would have to stop; she needed to start acting like a professional.

Her hand inched into her shirt and she fought the urge, forcibly stilling the hand. But her willpower lasted only a moment, and she reached inside and pulled out a piece of cloth. She pressed the soft garment to her face, against her cheek, then inhaled deeply of the scent that still lingered there.

She had taken only one thing from the Lady Jorden. On her last night there, right before she had climbed out the window, the camisole had caught her eye. It was lying on the dresser next to the decorative plate she had nearly broken. She had dragged her hand across the dresser, caught the strap with her finger, then tucked the undergarment into her pocket.

Syn examined the garment. It was exquisite. She loved to look at it, she loved to touch it, but most of all she loved the smell which held the scent of that woman. Syn's fascination with the article angered her, as did almost everything having to do with that noblewoman. Still, it did not stop her from tucking the cloth beneath her chin as she rolled over to go to sleep, clutching the garment in slumber like a child would a favorite, comforting blanket.

Chapter 7

Syn sat in the village square of Trygg, waiting for Raine. She was very conscious of the weight of the enchanted stone in her pocket. As described, the first job had been easy. It was a minor merchant who had inherited the stone from his father who had purchased it from a thief who had stolen it from an adventurer who had robbed a crypt where the stone had been sealed for centuries. None in the chain of possession had known what they held, including the merchant who had placed the stone in a plain box without even a lock. It had been a simple matter for Syn to enter his residence, elude him and his family, and secure the item without attracting the slightest attention. She carefully replaced the real stone with the fake one, then made a silent exit.

She wasn't certain how Raine would know that she had obtained the stone, but her instructions had been clear. Raine would meet her in Trygg after each successful theft. And so now she watched the bustling square from her vantage point on the balcony of the tavern where they had arranged to meet. Syn was not sure how she would recognize the woman, for Raine was certain to travel in disguise. But when she saw a hooded figure moving with deadly grace through the throng, like a wolf pacing through a herd of sheep, she knew that Raine had arrived. The hood tilted upward to the balcony, and the figure disappeared into the tavern below.

A short interval later, the figure came out onto the balcony. Raine glanced about, then lowered her hood. Once again, the thief impressed her, for it was an excellent meeting place, one practically invisible to those below but offering a clear view of the square from above. She set two glasses of mead onto the table between them, then sat down across from Syn and propped her feet up on a nearby chair.

Syn liked to look at Raine for she was incredibly gorgeous. But it was a comfortable admiration because it would never be acted upon. Not only was the blue-eyed creature clearly unobtainable, Syn was certain that dragon would eat her alive if she so much as tried.

"So, things went well?" Raine asked, taking a swig of mead. She had gotten rather spoiled flying about on Weynild, and this trip had been long and dusty.

"Yes," Syn said, and removed the stone from her pocket. It was wrapped in a small piece of soft leather which she held open.

"Perfect," Raine said, and removed a small box. "If you wouldn't mind putting it in here so I don't touch it."

Syn carefully set the stone in the silk-lined box, and Raine just as carefully closed it. She tucked the box into her pocket.

"Can I ask you how you knew that I had the stone?" Syn said.

Raine took a drink, thoughtful. "The stones speak to one another. When that one changed possession, the one on the bracelet began to glow brighter for a brief time, so we knew that you had it. It's making our meeting more convenient, but it also might make the next jobs more dangerous."

Syn took a drink, listening.

"I don't think it will be a factor in the next theft. That one will be more difficult simply because it's in a castle that's very secure. But the possessors of that stone are no more dangerous than that merchant. It's a job very suitable to your skills." Raine's expression darkened. "But the last stone is held by a sorceress who is very attuned to magic, and she'll know something is happening with the stones. In fact, she may know already." Raine shrugged. "We'll discuss that one when you're ready. It'll require some coordination."

Syn nodded and took a drink. She became aware that Raine was scrutinizing her.

"Are you sure nothing happened on this last theft?"

"No," Syn said, "why?"

"Because you suddenly have quite a bounty on your head, in fact, you have two of them."

"What?" Syn exclaimed.

"Yes," Raine said, "the empire has offered a reward of ten thousand gold for your capture, and the Guild of Thieves has offered fifteen."

Syn's thoughts raced. She knew exactly where those bounties had come from. "Damn her," she muttered, "I assure you it has nothing to do with the job, and nothing to do with theft at all."

Raine chuckled. "Ah," she said, understanding, "a woman. That explains why the description, at least that given to the Guild, was so specific."

"What do you mean?" Syn asked warily.

"It describes a scar on your thigh and some on your back and side."

"Damn her!" Syn said again. For once she had done absolutely nothing to bring this upon herself, and now she was in more trouble than she had ever been in. And Lagmann finally had an excuse to come after her full bore.

Raine actually felt sorry for the thief. She handed a pack to her across the table.

"I know you can steal anything you need, but here's some food and fresh clothing. It might help you lay low for a while."

Syn took the pack, grateful. "This won't affect my ability to get those stones," she said.

"I know that," Raine said, "and know that if you're captured, I'll not let you sit in jail." She chuckled once more. "I cannot, however, rescue you from some woman's bed."

Syn frowned. That was unfortunate, because the Lady Jorden's bed was far more dangerous to her than jail.

CHAPTER 8

Syn thought she was doing well, or at least relatively so, for she had only had sex with four women since leaving Trygg, well, five if you counted the cook who was so sexually repressed, she had climaxed for Syn's hand in less than a minute in exchange for a bowl of soup. But that tryst had been so brief Syn was not going to count that one, and therefore congratulated herself on her semi-celibacy. She had not stolen much, either, and marveled at how a little focus in her life tended to keep her out of trouble.

But this castle could be trouble, she thought, examining it from where she was sprawled beneath a mammoth oak tree. The castle was surrounded by a moat that was treacherously deep. She could probably swim across it, but the water level was far beneath the ledges on each side, and even if she could climb down into the water, it was unlikely she could climb back up the other side. There was a drawbridge that was open during the day, and there was a light but steady stream of people going in and out, but the guards checked everyone carefully. She could possibly sneak in, perhaps in the back of one of the wagons, but the guards were vigilant to examine even those. And even if she were to get into the castle courtyard, she would then stand out as someone who did not belong, unable to conduct the surveillance necessary to do the job successfully.

No, she thought, sighing aloud. This task was going to require extreme measures. She was going to have to get a real job.

Syn balanced the plates carefully. The head of the staff of the castle had been reluctant to hire someone unknown, but they were preparing for a very special dinner for a very special guest list, and the arrangements were becoming overwhelming. So, he had hired the young woman for several reasons, but more for her looks than any domestic abilities. This group, and one guest in particular, had certain "predilections," and if he had to throw this lass to the wolves to keep them satisfied, he would do so. Still, if she broke one more plate, he was going to have her head.

Syn tried to hide her irritation. This ridiculous job with its ridiculously petty requirements and its ridiculously foolish rituals made her glad for the fiftieth time in less than hour that she had chosen a different vocation. She could not believe that people spent their lives turning down beds "just so" and pouring drinks at "just such an angle" and from "just such a position." It made her want to steal everything in the castle, but she had to concentrate. As stupid as the duties required of her were, they had allowed her complete access to the palace and she knew exactly where the stone was. Tonight, right before the grand dinner, there would be an opportunity for her to make the switch, then hopefully she would be able to slip out without serving any of these pompous asses any food. Even if she had to go through with the dinner, she could slip out first thing in the morning under some pretext or another, and then she would be gone.

She felt her excitement grow, that pleasant tension that accompanied a well-laid plan minutes before its execution.

"You there, go up and make certain the east wing has sufficient linens."

Syn gladly complied. Apparently whatever guest was expected might stay a while because the preparations were quite elaborate. Or maybe rich people just went overboard on everything. She went up the stone steps and found that she was alone in the east wing. Again, her fingers itched to take things, but she denied herself the pleasure. She would not risk the discovery of some petty theft. Even if they did not suspect her, it would still heighten vigilance, and that she did not want. No, she would take only a single thing from this castle and then disappear.

The suite was both extravagant and luxurious, but one odd thing caught her eye. There was a marble bath that appeared to be carved from a single block of stone, a dwarven artifact if she had ever seen one. But that was not what caught her eye. Usually a cistern such as this would be filled with half-boiling, half-tepid water to create a warm bath. But this one had a large block of ice sitting in the center of it, one only now beginning to melt. Syn wondered how it had been transported from the mountains without melting, speculating that perhaps magic was involved. Or perhaps the ice had been created from magic. Either way, the rich were certainly strange in their beauty regimens.

Syn felt her excitement peak. She was already on the upper floors and had a perfectly good excuse for being here. Perhaps it was time to sneak into the west wing and switch the stones. She crossed the parapet that joined the wings, holding a stack of linens in her hands. If she was caught, she could claim she had misunderstood the direction of the head of housekeeping, which would be believed because he thought her an idiot.

There were a few servants milling about, but Syn easily eluded them, stepping from shadow-to-shadow without making a sound. She ducked around a corner, moved noiselessly down a carpeted hallway, then entered the room in which the stone was kept. It was in a chest that was double-locked, but neither lock was any challenge to her. She opened the lid of the chest and ignored the diamonds, emeralds, and pearls that lay before her, searching only for the milky stone. She found it, switched out the counterfeit, then quietly shut the chest, once again locking both locks. She then slipped silently back down the carpeted hallway, around the corner, then pushed through the door on to the parapet. The entire act had taken less than two minutes. She entered the east wing, fluffed a pillow with a significant degree of scorn, then started down the stairs, trying to suppress her elation. It sounded as if the guests were arriving, so she was probably stuck with serving dinner, but after that she would be gone.

Syn knew that something was wrong the moment she got to the bottom of the stairs. The chief of staff did not act out of the ordinary, he was nervous, but his nerves were for his dinner, that much was obvious. And the other members of the staff did not act unusual. But there were now two guards standing at the door, and they both looked pointedly at her. She thought furiously. Clearly, she had been found out, but they did not wish to make a commotion. Perhaps she could sneak out through the kitchen, then throw herself into the moat from one of the windows. But no sooner had she started in that direction than two more guards settled themselves at the kitchen door, again both looking pointedly at her.

Syn tried to calm herself, running through the various escape routes that she had identified. She pivoted toward the pantry, knowing there was a small exit from the storeroom into the courtyard where deliveries were made, but as she turned in that direction, another guard settled at that door. And as she turned about the large room, one-by-one, every exit was covered by a guard who made no move toward her, but simply watched her purposefully.

"Welcome, my lady. We're honored that you've finally accepted our invitation."

The words barely registered on Syn, but the response transformed her blood to ice.

"Thank you," the Lady Jorden said, "you have no idea how pleased I am to be here."

Syn turned to find a pair of blue-green eyes watching her with a malevolent intensity. She swallowed hard as the eyes burned into her, then leisurely traveled down her frame. The duke was unaware that he did not have his honored guest's full attention and continued to prattle on, but the head of the staff was very aware of the Lady Jorden's gaze. He inwardly thanked the gods he had decided to hire that striking lass, for there were rumors of the Lady's "needs" that had apparently not been rumors. He stepped forward and took Syn by the elbow.

"The Lady Jorden is an esteemed guest," the man said meaningfully. "You will see to her every desire."

Syn wanted to slap him. He knew nothing of the history between her and the Lady Jorden, yet here he was offering her up as some sort of sacrifice. It seemed everyone was willing to prostitute her to the noblewoman. But Syn did not have very many options right now.

"Of course," she said gritting her teeth and still under Jorden's malevolent gaze.

Syn walked across the room to Jorden and bowed slightly. "May I take the Lady's coat?" she said as servilely as she could.

"That's a different look for you," Jorden murmured, and Syn colored because she was wearing the starched white clothing of the rest of the servants. "Yes," Jorden continued a little louder, "you may."

Jorden removed her cloak and Syn's gaze immediately went to the low-cut neckline that revealed some stunning cleavage. As intimate as they had been, it was the most Syn had actually seen of her body and she could not stop a sharp intake of breath. She quickly looked away, but Jorden was well aware of her response as she handed her the coat. The chief of staff watched the exchange, delighted. He hurried back into the kitchen.

"You've arrived just in time for dinner," Syn said formally, "would you like me to take your things to your room while you dine?"

"No," Jorden said casually, "there's more than enough time for that later," and Syn colored again. "I think I would prefer that you serve me dinner," Jorden swung about and looked her full in the eye, "and remain within my sight." She examined the refined features of her captive, her gaze lingering on the long eyelashes, then on the lips. "And just so you understand your situation completely," she said, her voice lowering, "there are fifty imperial soldiers surrounding this castle and that many more of my personal guard. You don't even want to know how many of the Guild are here."

The duke approached and held out his arm which Jorden took. "The food smells divine," she commented, and he laughed heartily as Syn followed them into the dining room, seething.

Syn took her place across from Jorden, back from the table and slightly behind the guests where all good servants stood. And she stood at attention, forced to listen to the inane conversation of the wealthy as they talked of politics and commerce and other boring things. And then they talked of the Emperor which brought around the subject of the theft of his scepter which made the corners of Syn's mouth twitch, drawing Jorden's attention to her. And Jorden's eyes lingered upon her often, their blue-green depths expressing without subtlety what she was going to do to her. And try as she might, Syn could not stop her gaze from falling upon Jorden's breasts, behavior observed by the chief of staff who, under normal circumstance would have had Syn beaten, but now was so pleased he was fairly humming.

As distracting as Jorden's presence was, Syn forced herself to think through her circumstances. It was possible that she had not been discovered at all, that Jorden had simply tracked her down which meant the theft could still be a success. She had no idea how she was going to get out of her current predicament because it was very apparent the Lady Jorden was very angry with her. But as long as the stone went undiscovered, there was hope.

Dinner was over all too soon, and the duke immediately began fussing over Jorden.

"Thank you, your grace," Jorden said, "but I'm very tired from my journey and think I would like to retire early."

The duke was more than understanding, motioning to the chief of staff who immediately grabbed Syn by the elbow. "You will see the Lady Jorden to the east wing," he ordered.

"Of course, I will," Syn said darkly. She moved to Jorden's side and bowed stiffly once more. "May I show you to your room?"

"Yes," Jorden said, "you may."

Syn escorted Jorden up the steps. A few other staff members started to join them, but the chief of staff waved them off, shaking his head vigorously.

Syn's stomach fluttered as she walked into the east wing, then into Jorden's suite. Unsurprisingly, she was set upon by two of Jorden's guards, each who took an arm, restraining her. Jorden settled gracefully into a chair while they dragged Syn before her, forcing her to her knees.

"Search her," Jorden commanded, and Syn tensed but did not struggle. The guard quickly found the stone which he removed from her pocket and handed to Jorden. She held the milky gem in the palm of her hand.

"So, is this the real one or the fake?"

Syn jumped, startled, for it was clear Jorden knew far more than she thought.

"Your friend Vestein was remarkably cooperative."

This saddened Syn because she did not want Vestein to be hurt or even involved. She hoped he had given up the information immediately. Jorden was watching her with that practiced eye, the one that was good at identifying deception.

"So, this is the real one," she said, "and you've gotten what you came for."

Another guard approached carrying a pack, and Jorden set the gem on the side table.

"These are her things," the guard said.

Jorden looked at the rough-hewn pack with disdain. "Burn them."

Syn nearly got to her feet, but the guards held her down. Jorden watched the reaction with calculation.

"There's something in here that's dear to you."

In keeping with the game they were playing, Syn didn't have to say anything for Jorden merely read her mind. She motioned for the guard to hand her the pack and she began rummaging through it. She came out with a silver locket on a silver chain, very plain and simple. Syn swallowed hard.

"And what's this?" Jorden asked meaningfully. "A gift from a lover? A girlfriend?"

Syn stared at the locket, unwilling to give Jorden anything else to hold over her but more unwilling to see the locket meet harm.

"It was my mother's," Syn said. "It's the only thing I have from her."

Jorden stared at her a long moment, then undid the clasp on the necklace and placed it around her own neck. The locket settled on the cushion of the swell of her breasts, nestled in the cleavage.

"Then I will keep it for you," Jorden said. She returned to rummaging through the pack, and a strange expression crossed her face as she pulled one of her own camisoles from it.

"What is this?"

Syn turned away, her cheeks hot with shame. She could not meet Jorden's stare.

"Are you falling in love with me?" Jorden said mockingly.

"Of course not!" Syn replied.

Jorden had regretted her mocking tone the instant it came out, but the vehemence of Syn's response made her wish it had been even more so. She threw the pack at the guard. "Burn it," she said. Syn turned at the command, but her eyes did not follow the pack which she obviously cared nothing about but rather the camisole that Jorden still held in her hand, and she appeared relieved. Jorden, who thought she understood this woman perfectly, at the moment didn't understand her at all, and it made her furious.

"Bind her," she said, "and then put her in."

Syn began struggling but she was no match for the two guards, and certainly no match when the third returned. They bound her hands then lifted her bodily from the ground and carried her to the marble tub. It was no longer filled with the block of ice, but now was filled with freezing water. They plunged her in and her whole body felt as if it were twisting into a knot as she doubled up from the painful cramping. They pushed her head beneath the surface and the pain intensified as the blood vessels constricted under the onslaught of cold.

Jorden watched the scene impassively. The cold would be painful, but it would not cause any permanent harm. She wanted to beat Syn, but that would damage her and that was not what she wanted. She merely wanted to punish her and to break her down further.

Finally, they brought Syn gasping to the surface and pulled her from the water. She was shaking as if from ague and could not control her limbs. She could not stand, so they laid her on the ground, and she curled up into a ball, violently trembling.

"You may go," she said to the guards, and they left. Normally they would not leave their mistress with such a prisoner, but that pathetic ball on the floor wasn't going anywhere.

"Helga," Jorden said, and her personal servant stepped from the shadows. "Strip her and put her in front of the fire."

Helga nodded and methodically went about her mistress's command. The woman's clothes were difficult to remove, not only because they were wet and plastered to her, but because her limbs were stiff and immovable. Helga eventually decided to cut them from her, her face expressionless at the blue skin beneath the clothes. She also cut the bindings on her wrists. Helga helped the benumbed figure to the fire, who could barely walk and collapsed on the soft fur that had been placed there. She then stoked the flames, bowed to her mistress, and departed. Nothing shocked Helga. She was well-used to the perversity of her mistress's desires, although really, she had never quite seen the Lady Jorden so obsessed with anyone before.

Jorden removed her own clothes and pulled a blanket from the bed, wrapping it about her. Syn lay on the white fur, curled into a ball, her back to her, and Jorden gazed on that beautiful backside and those beautiful scars. She lay down on the fur behind Syn and wrapped herself about her form, pulling the blanket over both of them. She enjoyed the intense cold of Syn's skin, and her nipples hardened against her back. Syn still trembled and shook, but Jorden pulled her close and murmured to her soothingly. And somehow, although Jorden had been the architect of Syn's misery, Syn slowly relaxed in her arms and finally fell into an exhausted sleep.

Hours later, Jorden awoke, wrapped about Syn. The fire had burned down to embers, but the room was very warm. She looked down at her captive lover, surprised to see that Syn had turned in her sleep and was now facing her. Their lower limbs were intertwined and Syn had thrown her arm about Jorden in her slumber, her face buried in her chest. The unconscious surrender pleased her, and she vowed to be more patient with Syn. She did not want to harm her and she certainly did not wish to damage her further, but she was intent on unlocking the desires she knew lay deep beneath Syn's surface, desires that were undoubtedly a perfect counterbalance to her own.

CHAPTER 9

Syn awoke to wonderful warmth and softness and for the longest stretch had no idea where she was. Perhaps it was because her current condition was so completely opposite that which she had been in prior to sleep, but it was several minutes before she could remember much of anything. When events did finally return to her, she could not believe she was wrapped in a blanket lying on a soft fur in front of a fireplace as if she were in some chalet on holiday.

She rolled over and examined the room. She was alone. She had no doubt that there were guards at the door, and there were no other doors or windows in this room, so escape wasn't presently an option. She had no clothes on, so that was an issue, but only for a moment. When she stood, she could see that clothing had been laid out on the bed for her. It was as stylish and appropriate as what Jorden had chosen before, so she knew that the woman had left it for her. There was also food on the table, not the food that the servants ate, but the food that had been reserved for the most honored guest in the house. Syn sat down to roasted pheasant stuffed with almonds, orange marmalade jam, freshly churned butter and fresh baked bread. There was a flagon of water that was cool and a cup of tea that was hot, and she drank both. Then, because she had nothing better to do, she sat in one of the chairs before the fire and before long, fell asleep.

Jorden came in, tensed when she saw that Syn was not lying on the floor any longer, then relaxed when she saw her asleep in the chair. She settled across from her. She was pleased to see Syn wearing the clothing she had laid out and not engaged in some foolish, meaningless mutiny. Every acquiescence, no matter how small, was a step further down the path she wished her to take.

Syn stirred and opened her eyes. In that space before memory or sense could take hold, she noted how gorgeous Jorden looked today in her short jacket and gown, a stylish ensemble generally worn by noblewomen when they rode horses. Then both memory and sense returned, and she frowned.

"Such a look," Jorden commented. "So many crave my attention and affection, yet you run from me."

"Perhaps that's why you chase me," Syn said sarcastically, "perhaps if I stopped running you would no longer want me."

"Perhaps," Jorden said unapologetically. "Why don't you stop running and we'll see?"

"All right, I'll just let you do with me as you will, you'll grow tired of me, and this will end."

Jorden's eyes gleamed. "Then you'll let me do with you as I will?"

Syn shifted uncomfortably in the chair. "No," she said, backing from that tack in a hurry. Jorden's response alone told her that idea was dangerous.

"How unfortunate," Jorden said. "Still, the chief of staff here has transferred your employment contract to me. I just have to figure out how to get you to Grenjad."

Syn rolled her eyes. "I don't have an employment contract with that buffoon."

"Should I tell him then that you were working here only so you could steal something?"

Syn rubbed her eyelids and temples. She had forgotten what a bad situation she was in. And the comment about returning her to Grenjad stoked her unease as well. She looked to the remains of the meal she had eaten. It would be a simple matter for Jorden to drug her food; she would have to be careful. If she got her back into that fortress of a house, escape would be very difficult.

Jorden's inspection of her grew pointed, and Syn's unease increased more. She braced herself for one of Jorden's "casual" questions that never was.

"So," Jorden began, "how many women have you been with since me?"

Ah, there it was, Syn thought. She desperately wanted to lie to Jorden but the odds of her success weren't good as she had accomplished the feat exactly once. "A half-dozen or so," Syn admitted, wondering why it was an "admission" since it was none of Jorden's concern. Syn could see the flash of anger in those blue-green eyes, although the follow-up question was coolly spoken.

"Which is it?" Jorden asked, "A half-dozen? Or a half-dozen or so?"

"Or so," Syn said, her tone again involuntarily confessional.

Jorden leaped to her feet and Syn immediately mirrored the action in self-preservation. By the gods, this woman had a temper. Jorden picked up a book and flung it at her head, a missile that Syn barely deflected by raising her hands to protect herself. The book was followed by another, then by a plate, then finally by a vase that shattered loudly when it struck the wall. The only thing that saved Syn from taking the vase in the head was the fact she tripped on the fur rug and smacked her head on the mantle of the fireplace, then went down in a daze. The noise was enough to make the guards run in, but they stopped when they saw that their mistress had the situation well in hand.

"I beg your pardon, my lady," the guard said. "We thought you were in danger."

"I'm fine," Jorden replied, menace in her tone, and the guards were happy the menace was not directed at them. They quickly bowed out, almost feeling sorry for the bemused woman on the floor. Jorden stalked over to Syn and pulled her away from the fireplace, then pushed her onto her back on the fur rug. And Syn did not struggle, partially because she was dazed, and partially because this woman had some sort of power over her that was beyond reason. Jorden straddled her and pinned her arms above her head.

"You are the most infuriating woman I've ever met," Jorden said, and Syn had no idea how she had wound up on this side of the conversation. Jorden inspected the body beneath her. "I should tie you up and beat you right now."

Jorden saw the flash of fear on Syn's face and calmed herself. Not now. And not this way. Instead, she leaned down and kissed the small cut that had formed on Syn's forehead, completely confusing her captive. Jorden returned to the green eyes, noting that the fear had been replaced by bewilderment.

"And how many of those women made you come?" Jorden whispered to her.

Syn tried to hold her gaze. Tried, and failed. She looked away, the muscles in her jaw visibly working.

"None," Jorden whispered triumphantly. "Not one."

Jorden released one of her wrists and Syn could feel the hand slip inside her shirt, then down inside her pants.

"No," Syn said, trying to twist away, but Jorden held her firmly.

"You will not tell me no," Jorden instructed, slipping her fingers inside Syn while stroking her with her thumb. "You will not pull away from me," she said, kissing her, then biting her neck, the fingers and thumb hard at work, "and you will come for me every single time."

The command itself was enough to bring Syn to climax as her hips writhed beneath the hand that treated her so mercilessly so effortlessly. This woman had to be a demon, for she could wrench orgasms from Syn with hardly a touch, a bite, and an imperative word. And then she could prolong the orgasm by continuing to play and bite and caress until every bit of ecstasy was wrung from the frenzied motion of Syn's hips. And then she would bury her tongue in her mouth in a deep, probing final kiss, one as searing and dominating as everything that came before it.

"Mmm," Jorden said, gazing down at her. "That's better." She leaned back and straightened Syn's clothing, then stood upright. "I'm going to make arrangements for us to leave for Grenjad."

Syn lay on the rug staring up at the ceiling.

Several days passed and Syn spent them all in the captivity of Jorden's room. Helga brought her food at regular intervals while Jorden spent time fulfilling whatever social obligations the visit had incurred. Apparently, no one in the household thought Syn's absence strange, or perhaps they had just determined her expendable.

And then Jorden would return and spend extended spans with her toy, always methodically, insistently, seductively wrenching at least one orgasm from Syn, and more often than not, more than one. She preyed upon Syn's weaknesses, noting every little gesture and glance. When Helga mentioned drawing a hot bath, Jorden noted Syn's longing glance toward the marble cistern and had the bath drawn. She then spent an hour leisurely washing every inch of Syn's body, paying particular attention to the scars that so mesmerized her, then brought Syn to a shuddering climax as her fingers went to work beneath the surface of the warm, soapy water.

Jorden still would not let Syn touch her and Syn had yet to see any more of her body than the cleavage the well-cut gowns revealed. But she would allow Syn to kiss her, or at least return her kiss when Jorden was on top of her, and Syn often found herself doing so hungrily, passionately, it providing the only outlet for her growing desperate desire to bring Jorden pleasure. Syn would not know how many times her kiss alone had nearly pushed Jorden over the edge. She would not know that Jorden had another room but a few doors down in which she went to pleasure herself to relieve the intense desire Syn inspired. She knew only that Jorden watched her, calculating, as if she were waiting for something, something that frightened Syn but something they were moving towards inexorably.

Syn wondered if Raine was waiting for her in Trygg. If the stones spoke to one another as she said, surely, they would have known she had obtained the second. She wondered what they would think when she did not make the pre-arranged meeting and the possibilities bothered her greatly. Normally she cared nothing of what others thought of her, but it disturbed her to think that Raine would be disappointed in her, or worse, that she would think Syn had betrayed her.

Which is why, when a thunderous roar shook the castle to its very foundation the next morning, Syn was not certain whether to be happy or terrified. She knew instantly the sound, for it had deafened her outside of the cottage in the wilderness. And it was followed by tumult, the sounds of running and screaming, men yelling, soldiers shouting orders, all of which were drowned out each time the dragon's roar echoed across the valley.

Syn went to the door and cautiously pressed it open. The guards were down the hallway, oblivious to her. They were cowering in the door that led to the parapet stretching between the wings of the castle. A few sought to fire arrows but were shaking so badly they could barely notch them. Syn moved out into the hallway and peered down the top of the stairs. There was a huge group of soldiers and guards gathered at the base, so that was not an option. She moved stealthily down the hallway toward the parapet, but the stealth was unnecessary. No one was paying the slightest bit of attention to her in the chaos. She walked right past the cowering guards and outside onto the walkway.

A fiery red dragon was wreaking havoc on the surrounding countryside. Wildlife was running in every direction while the domesticated herd animals scattered directly behind them. Syn swore she saw a pig trample a wolf in its terrified flight. Soldiers flailed about, running into one another or trying to hide in ditches or behind rocks. A few intrepid souls were trying to stage a rally, but the dragon swooped down, knocking them all flat on their backs. It was almost comical, especially since, at least to Syn's eye, the dragon wasn't really doing any damage. In fact, it looked to be far more of a diversion than an attack. She caught movement out of the corner of her eye and looked down. There was a figure standing on the far side of the moat waving to her. It took her a moment to realize it was Raine, and that she was motioning to her.

"By the gods that's a splendid creature," Jorden murmured, and Syn was startled to find Jorden standing right next to her. Jorden seemed to become aware of Syn's presence at the same time and turned her attention from the dragon.

"What are you doing out here?" she said with a hint of threat.

Syn stared at her, then without thinking, pulled her into her arms. She kissed her fully, passionately, desperately, then pushed her away.

"I came to say goodbye," Syn said, then before Jorden could grab her, she leaped to the edge of the parapet and flung herself off the side. She twisted in the air, trying to adjust her body position to something that wouldn't kill her on impact and prayed that she had judged the water correctly. She seemed to fall for an eternity, and when at last she hit the water she was certain she had missed for it felt like solid rock. But then she was scrambling for the surface, gasping for breath, and although every part of her body hurt, she began pulling herself through the murky depths. And then Raine was there at the water's edge, hand extended to pull her out.

"What in the world was that?" Raine said in disbelief.

"You motioned for me to jump," Syn said.

"Not to jump, you fool," Raine said. She pointed up to the edge of the parapet. "There's a rope!"

And as Syn looked up, there was indeed a rope hanging from an arrow that no doubt Raine had impaled so perfectly and securely with that magnificent bow.

"Oh," Syn said, "a rope."

Raine helped her to her feet. "Did you break anything?"

"I think I broke everything," Syn said. She shook her head. "No, I'll be fine. Let's get out of here."

Raine practically carried Syn up the rocky slope, and there were two horses there, the only two beasts that weren't running amok at the moment. In truth, the beasts were almost placid, as if it were not unusual that there was a gigantic magical reptile flying about, roaring so loudly it made the ground quake while it incinerated everything in sight. Raine helped Syn up onto one of the horses.

"Are you sure you can ride?" Raine asked, concerned as Syn nearly fell from the horse.

"Yes," Syn said as Raine mounted her own horse. She took one last look at the figure standing on the parapet, one who although too far away to actually be seen, appeared to be gazing down at her coolly in sharp contrast to everything around her. "Let's go."

Jorden watched Syn pull herself from the water with the help of some-one. It was difficult to tell if it was a man or a woman and Jorden thought if might have been an elf because the creature moved with a deadly grace and was inordinately strong for his or her size. Jorden's eyes flicked to the dragon still wheeling about the sky, the dragon that seemed to be losing interest in its current role in creating the drama beneath it. Her little thief had some very interesting clients right now.

That thought brought Jorden back to the passionate embrace and farewell, and her hands went to her pockets. She grit her teeth, angry but not the least bit surprised to find the milky stone gone, filched by Syn when she held her in her arms and distracted her with the kiss. Her anger simmered as her hand went to her throat and the other checked the opposite pocket, but then the anger transitioned into perplexity.

She looked down, fingering Syn's locket that still hung securely about her neck while the other hand came from the pocket empty. Syn's skill as a pickpocket was unmatched, so why in the world had she taken her camisole and left her mother's locket?

CHAPTER 10

Raine carried Syn through the empty tavern. She thought they might be here for a while, so Raine had rented the entire lodge out indefinitely. The barkeep looked as if he might ask her some questions, but then she handed him enough gold to buy the tavern outright, and his mouth clamped shut.

"I'm expecting a few visitors," Raine said, "they'll ask for me by name."

The barkeep nodded. He would do whatever this one said.

Raine carried Syn up the stairs and got her settled into bed. Raine could tell she was in pain but Syn had not once complained on the way there. Raine pulled a few herbs from her pack and went to the bowl of water left by the maid. She made two mixtures, one a potion and one a poultice. Syn drank the potion, which did not taste nearly as bad as she had expected and seemed to take the edge from her pain.

"I'm going to need to see your ribs," Raine said, holding the poultice in her hand. She could tell by the way that Syn was holding herself that the ribs were injured. Hopefully they were only bruised and not broken.

"That's not necessary," Syn said uncomfortably.

"What? Are you shy all of a sudden? Just lift your shirt, I won't look."

Syn lifted the edge of her shirt slightly, but it was not enough for Raine to even see her bottom rib and she frowned at her. She could, however, see the pattern of fine lines on Syn's side, and it dawned upon her why Syn was self-conscious.

"Would you like to see mine?" Raine asked.

"What?"

Raine set the poultice aside and stood up. "Here, let me show you." She pulled her shirt over her head so that her back was exposed and Syn stared in amazement as a series of intricate blue and gold markings appeared. Raine truly had one of the most beautiful backs she had ever seen, muscular with no thickness tapering in a "V" down to a slender waist. But the markings were also gorgeous, some type of coloration woven beneath the skin itself.

"Is there something going on here?" Weynild said as she sauntered into the room, her casual tone indicating how implausible that would be.

"We're sharing scars," Raine said, turning to kiss Weynild over her shoulder as the silver-haired woman ran a caress down the markings on her back.

"Those are scars?" Syn asked.

"Yes," Raine said. Few would recognize Scinterian markings because most thought the warrior race had died out centuries before. "My people had a ceremony whose purpose was to inflict pain, and the markings are the badge of honor resulting from that ceremony."

"Why did they wish to cause you pain?"

"The idea is for the young to experience pain so intense that all else in their life will pale in comparison."

"And did it work?" Syn asked slowly.

"I assure you," Raine said, "it most definitely did."

"It also gave her a most wonderful tolerance for pain," Weynild said, settling into a chair as she cast Raine a scorching glance. The two had a way about them, an intimacy that smoldered beneath the surface all the time and could ignite into flame at any moment. It was remarkable to watch, because even though Syn was sitting there, it was as if no one else was in the room, or in fact anywhere in the world, but them. Raine politely broke that spell by casting Syn a wolfish grin.

"That's important when your lover is a dragon." She pulled her shirt down and moved to Syn's side. "Now let me see your ribs."

Syn pulled up the shirt and Raine pressed lightly in several places. "I think they're bruised," she said, "but they don't feel broken. It'll hurt for a while, but you should be better in a few days. Here," she said, pressing the poultice to the injured area, "hold this in place."

Syn pressed the poultice to her side, then adjusted her position so it would stay. She became very conscious of a pair of golden eyes staring at her.

"So," Weynild said drily, "still fucking your way across Arianthem?"

"No!" Syn exclaimed, then corrected, "Well, yes. But that's not what happened." She pulled the enchanted gem from her pocket. "I stole the stone with no problem." The stone was wrapped in a cloth and she handed it carefully to Raine. Raine handled it just as carefully, touching only the cloth, and then removed a small box from her pocket and placed the stone within. Syn was watching her closely.

"Um, I'll take that," she said, nodding to the cloth. Raine lifted it up to hand it back, and it unfolded, causing her to gaze at the camisole in amused consternation. Weynild made a rude noise from her corner.

"Just give it here," Syn said with a black look, and the dragon muffled laughter.

"As I was saying," Syn continued, "The theft was perfect. I joined the castle staff, worked for a few days, scouted the interior, then made the switch undiscovered."

"Then what happened?" Raine asked.

"That woman happened!" Syn exploded. "She found me and next I knew I was kidnapped again."

"She seems quite enamored with you," Raine said.

"I don't think enamored is the word."

"Regardless, she is persistent," Raine said. "Do you think you can stay out of her clutches long enough for the final job?"

"I intend to stay out of her clutches for the rest of my life."

Raine looked at the thief, at the camisole she held wrapped about her hand, then looked to Weynild who also had a look of deep skepticism at the pronouncement. Neither of them believed that for a moment.

"Well," Raine said, "we're going to need some assistance on this final stone, so I'm waiting for some reinforcements. I'm torn on this plan, though. Part of me thinks I should go get it myself."

"And why don't you?" Syn asked curiously. She could understand why they had contracted with her to get the first two; they were ideal circumstances for a thief. But if this one was complicated, then perhaps it would be better for Raine to go in cleanly.

Raine sighed. "Don't get me wrong. Although I'm not as stealthy as you, it's likely I could get very close to the stone. But I have no doubt the sorceress now carries the stone upon her. And although I would kill her without hesitation," and Raine's words were so matter-of-fact they sent a chill up Syn's spine, "it's possible she would destroy the stone before I could get to it. And that would render the bracelet useless."

"So you need someone 'non-threatening' to get near the stone."

"I won't sacrifice you," Raine said firmly, "if that's what you're thinking. I would rather the stone be destroyed. But if it can be obtained, then that would be my first wish."

"I know you won't abandon me," Syn said, "you rescued me from that woman's bed even though you said you wouldn't."

Raine smiled. "And know this, the reinforcement that I'm offering you is no small resource. I'm pairing you with the only person in Arianthem that is possibly stealthier than you."

CHAPTER 11

Raine sat in the empty tavern, her feet propped on a table, her chair tilted back against the wall. She was on her third tankard of mead, but it was having little effect. She was eying a bottle of amber liquid above the bar, contemplating asking the barkeep if it was indeed an amber sting. But she would wait for her love to return, just in case it was that mythic liqueur. That drink had a fairly pronounced effect on her that she did not want to waste.

A hooded figure came through the door and Raine could tell by the way she moved it was whom she was waiting for. This one would not leave tracks in newly fallen snow. The barkeep made a move to run the figure off, but Raine waved to him and he returned to the bar. Raine did notice, however, that the figure was accompanied by two others, which was unexpected. The figure approached, gave a short bow in the Tavinter custom, and removed her hood.

"Hello, Skye," Raine said.

Skye smiled a brilliant smile, her hazel eyes bright with pleasure. "Hello, Raine," she said, clasping her forearm.

Raine examined the lovely young woman, pleased at the assessment. It had not been that long ago that Skye had been desperately ill and Raine had played a pivotal role in her rescue. But now she appeared healthy, her tan skin glowing, her light hair full and lively on her head, her cheeks still sharp and refined but with a blush of fitness on them now.

"Thank you for coming," Raine said, "I was reluctant to ask you to do this for many reasons, including the fact that it's a sordid affair to involve the ruler of the Tavinter."

"Hmm," Skye said, "then you're probably going to be less than happy with who I brought with me."

The two figures flanking Skye removed their hoods, revealing two women as stunning as Skye. The one on the left had flashing dark eyes and dark hair.

"Your Highness," Raine said wryly, and Dallan bowed to her in the Ha'kan greeting of one royalty to another. Dallan was the heir to the Ha'kan throne, the Princess of an all-female race of warriors, scholars, and priestesses, a race that rivaled the Empire in terms of military and political power.

"Raine," Dallan said formally, "and I believe you know Rika as well."

Raine turned to the other woman, a very handsome lady who acted as Dallan's right hand. "Ah yes," Raine said, "the future First General of the Ha'kan." Raine examined her. "You look even larger than the last time I saw you."

"Thank you," Rika said, trying to hide her pleasure at the compliment.

Raine shifted her attention back to Dallan, who despite her attempt to maintain her royal dignity wilted beneath Raine's amused stare. "You didn't expect us to let her come alone, did you?"

"I don't even know why I'm surprised," Raine said. "Please, have a seat." She waved to the barkeep, who ran over to her side.

"My friends will need rooms," Raine said, "but right now they need some drinks." She leaned toward Skye. "You are old enough to drink now, aren't you?'

"Barely," Rika commented, and Skye threw her a black look.

"Yes," Skye said, "I can have a drink."

Dallan settled into her seat, casting a nervous glance about her. Raine was entertained because Dallan was fearless, an exceptional warrior and an outstanding leader. There were very few things that caused her anxiety.

"So," Dallan said, "is Talan here?"

Raine took a drink to hide her smile. Weynild's true name was Talan'alaith'illaria. "She's out and about, but will be back soon."

"Ah, wonderful," Dallan said, her tone opposite her words.

Raine turned her attention to Skye.

"The other reason why I was reluctant to ask for your help is that this does involve Ingrid."

Skye paled slightly and Raine thought perhaps she would abandon her plans. But Skye squared her shoulders and sat upright in her seat.

"I welcome the opportunity to even that score."

Raine examined her at length. Ingrid was the immensely powerful sorceress who had kidnapped Skye and then abused her in many perverse ways, leading to her deathly illness. To this day, Raine was not certain that Skye knew why Ingrid had taken her, but it was unlikely that Ingrid's motivation would change, which would mean that Skye would be in immeasurable danger. But Skye was unmatched in her ability to infiltrate any facility.

"All right," Raine said, "I'll be there if needed. I'll not leave you to her should you be discovered."

"Nor I," Dallan said emphatically, and Rika made a derisive noise that indicated she would be there as well.

"Good," said Raine, "we'll discuss the details more in depth once my thief recovers." Raine looked up. "And I see my love has returned."

Dallan started and looked as if she wished to bolt from her chair. The response would normally have made Rika laugh, but she, too, was in awe and fear of the striking silver-haired woman. And she was also uncomfortably aroused because the dragon queen wore sensuality draped about her like a cloak. Although the Ha'kan were known for unrestrained sexual appetites and a total lack of monogamy, the sexual prowess and lust of the dragons was legendary. The fact that the three of them had met the dragon when they were little more than children at the Academy had made her impression upon them all the more powerful.

"Oh my," Weynild said, glancing at the young women as she settled into the seat next to Raine. Dallan remembered her manners, stood, and gave the proper greeting as she had done with Raine, one royal to another, and Rika and Skye stood as well. The golden eyes flicked from one to the next as all three retook their seats, at which time her eyes returned to the Princess.

"Does your mother know where you are?"

Raine hid her smile in her tankard of mead. Weynild was unrelenting with these three, especially the Ha'kan heir. Dallan looked indignant, sought furiously for a retort, then came up with nothing.

"No," she said angrily, and Weynild laughed out loud. Her gaze settled on Skye.

"And how is our little Tavinter doing?" she asked.

"I'm fine, thank you," Skye said, calm beneath the woman's intent inspection, impressing the dragon. Skye's physical attraction to Raine and Weynild was as powerful as her companions', but it was tempered with a fierce loyalty and adoration.

"And are you prepared to face the sorceress again?"

Weynild noted the same slight paling that Raine had observed, but the girl's voice was calm.

"Yes."

The golden eyes assessed her. The girl seemed unaware of why exactly the sorceress was so interested in her, but still she would test her.

"And you've been practicing magic?" Weynild queried.

"Yes," Skye said with enthusiasm, "I'm not very good. I've been working with Gimle only a short stint. But I've made some progress. It's most unexpected."

"She's immensely talented," Rika said, unwilling to let Skye sell herself short.

"I see," Weynild said. She felt the intent survey of the Princess and slid her glance that way. Most of the time Dallan would have been unable to meet those gleaming golden eyes, but now she stared at the dragon very hard. Skye had shown no propensity or interest in magic, and yet suddenly Dallan's mother, Queen Halla, had suggested she might possess the skill. It occurred to her that the Queen had made the suggestion in very close proximity to her private conversations with Talan.

The golden eyes returned to Skye. "It would be dangerous for you to use any magic in this quest. The sorceress will sense you, so I suggest you rely on your traditional skills."

Skye nodded. "I'm not good enough to use magic, anyway. I'll gladly rely on my sword and bow."

"Hopefully you'll need neither and can sneak in and out," Raine said. "Syn is excellent in a city, as good as you are in nature," she said to Skye. "But she's helpless in the forest and the sorceress is holed up in a tower deep in the heart of the Black Woods. I will help get you through the forest, because I understand Hyr'rok'kin have been gathering there. But I can't get too close or Ingrid will destroy the stone."

"And you don't think Ingrid will destroy it if she sees us?"

"No," Raine said, "Syn is not particularly threatening and you, well..."

"My presence will distract her," Skye said with discomfort.

"Yes," Raine said. "I could send Syn in there alone, but Ingrid will kill her if she discovers her. You at least can protect yourself. And you won't have to for long because if you need me, I'll be there."

"But how will you know?" Dallan asked.

"I will know," Raine said simply, and although the words themselves were not reassuring, the tone was utterly so.

"But then she'll destroy the stone," Skye said, "and all will have been for naught."

"If it happens, so be it," Raine said. "That's not my hope, but I'll not sacrifice you or Syn for a bauble."

Skye knew this was not a bauble. This stone was greatly important to Raine and Weynild, that much was clear. She would do her best to see that they remained undiscovered.

"Barkeep!" Raine called across the empty tavern, and the man ran over. "We'll have those drinks, now."

Weynild eyed the bottle sitting on the shelf above the bar. "Is that an amber sting I see?"

"Yes," the barkeep said, and Weynild cast a sultry glance in Raine's direction. "You're familiar with the legend?" he asked

Neither Raine nor Weynild spoke, but Rika did. "I'm not," she volunteered, encouraging the barkeep to continue.

"It is said that the amber sting is a gift given to the Scinterians by the dragons of old."

Rika, Dallan, and Skye all looked to Raine and Weynild, for although the barkeep was unaware of the fact, he was in the presence of the only Scinterian left in the world, as well as one of the very last dragons.

"The liqueur is so strong it allows the Scinterians to breathe fire just as their dragon brethren. But it's a deadly drink," he warned.

Weynild regarded Raine expectantly.

"You know how I am, my love," Raine said, "that drink will heighten my libido and lower my inhibitions."

Without pause Weynild turned to the barkeep. "I'll pay you a small fortune to double the strength."

The man was shocked. "That will kill her!" he exclaimed.

"I assure you," Weynild said, "she is quite indestructible. But I cannot guarantee the same of your room upstairs."

The barkeep returned with the drink and Raine downed it without effort, greatly astonishing him. Then, without further delay, the dragon and her lover started upstairs. Although enamored with her love, Raine managed to politely wave goodbye to her companions while for Talan, they had ceased to exist.

"I am wet the entire time I'm around those two."

"Rika!" Dallan exclaimed, although her shocked exclamation was less shocked than obligatory. She would not have put it so crudely, but the silver-haired woman and her blue-eyed lover had the same effect on her.

"My," Skye breathed out. She had eagerly adopted the non-monogamous ways of the Ha'kan, but that pair was stunningly romantic.

Just then a rakishly attractive woman came down the stairs. Her shoulder-length hair hung fetchingly about her face, softening sharply good-looking features. She was holding her hand to her side as if she were in pain.

"Hello," she mumbled to the three women sitting and watching her. These had to be Raine's reinforcements because no one else was allowed in the bar. She felt a surge of irritation looking at them. Was everyone on this quest going to be gorgeous? They were going on a mission, not a damned beauty pageant. She felt like a troll.

"Hmm," Rika said with interest.

"Stop it," Skye said. "Raine said she's easily distracted."

Syn walked to the bar, pushed the barkeep out of the way, and poured herself some hard liquor. Mead was not going to cut it right now. "Thank you," she muttered to the barkeep, who watched her with some disapproval as she made her way across the bar. She sprawled into the chair that Raine had vacated.

"You're friends of Raine?"

"Yes," Skye said, feeling a little thrill at the association. Undying servants was a more apt description.

"Hmmph," Syn said noncommittally. The little beauty with the hazel eyes was the youngest of the three, and she actually wasn't that little. She was probably Syn's height, if not taller. But compared to the other two, she looked small. The one on the left had the chiseled, perfect features of nobility, possibly even royalty, with long dark hair and intense dark eyes. The one on the right was handsome and wore her hair shorter, but she, too, possessed the refined features of aristocracy. Syn thought she was probably older than all three by a few years.

"What happened to you?" Skye asked, noting her pained movement. "I thought Raine said there were no problems with the first two stones."

Syn shook her head. "This was not from the stones, that caper went off without a hitch." Syn shifted uncomfortably. "I got this from jumping off the parapet of a castle into a moat. After thirty or forty feet, water is not so soft."

Skye's eyes glowed. "That sounds like fun."

Syn looked at her. This must be the insane one, or at least the one Syn had labeled insane from Raine's description of her. "Yes," she said, "it would have been more fun had I seen the rope Raine left for me."

"And what were you escaping from?" Dallan asked.

Syn's expression darkened and Rika leaned forward. She knew that look. "It was a woman, was it not?"

"Yes," Syn said, "a woman who keeps kidnapping me."

"Does she harm you?" Skye asked, concerned.

"No, no, not really," Syn said. "She dunked me in some very cold water, but that was more unpleasant than anything else. It really didn't do me any harm."

Skye glanced to Dallan. "So, what does this woman do with you?" Dallan asked.

"Well," Syn said, shifting uncomfortably but not due to pain, "she has sex with me."

"Ah," Rika said, leaning back with understanding. "She forces you to service her against your will."

"No," Syn said slowly, "No, not really. Actually, she services me."

Rika looked to Skye who looked to Dallan.

"She is hideously ugly?" Dallan suggested.

"No, no," Syn said, even more slowly, her gaze distant, "she is actually quite beautiful."

Dallan sat back, frowning, and Rika was even blunter. "I don't understand non-Ha'kan women," she muttered.

"Nor I," Syn murmured, seeing a pair of blue-green eyes and knowing she was talking as much about herself as she was the Lady Jorden.

CHAPTER 12

Syn was feeling much better. Raine had been right. The ribs were sore, but it had only taken a few days for her to heal. Now she could move about with a minimum of discomfort. And the few days in the tavern had been some of the most enjoyable of her life. Weynild had left and Raine kept to herself, but the two Ha'kan and the Tavinter were warm and funny, offering little in judgment toward her but teasing her unmercifully about her infatuation with the mysterious Lady Jorden. They did not share much personally, but Syn could tell they were all very important people, which made her sad because she would have enjoyed maintaining their friendship when the job was done, an idea that previously would have never crossed her mind. But she knew that these well-bred young ladies would part ways with her the minute things were finished.

She was curious about the relationship between the three. She had heard stories of the Ha'kan but did not understand their society. At first, she thought that Dallan and Skye were a couple, then she became convinced that it was actually Skye and Rika who were together, but then she became completely confused because it seemed that Dallan and Rika were the couple. And their sleeping arrangements provided no clue because they stayed in a single room with a single large bed. The whole thing was baffling to Syn.

"I'm going to stretch my legs," Syn said.

Skye glanced up from the table where she was reading. Her studies from the Academy had been interrupted and she was still trying to make up for lost time. "Are you sure that's wise?" she said, "Raine said you have quite a bounty on your head."

Syn felt a little flush of shame, but Skye clearly cared nothing about the bounty. Syn could not know it, but Skye had once had a far higher bounty than that, one placed by the Ha'kan Princess who now shared her bed.

"I'll cover myself," Syn said, "and I won't be gone that long."

"All right then," Skye said, returning to her book. "I'll see you when you get back."

The fresh air felt good. Syn felt good. She was nervous about the upcoming mission, but also excited. She normally liked to work alone, but she was grateful she had competent help on this one. And oddly, as she walked about the merchant square, she had no desire to steal anything. She passed jewels, necklaces, amulets, bracelets, rings, every type of valuable, and not once did she feel that itch in her palm to pluck the item from its satin pillow or velvet-lined case. It was strange, almost exhilarating to Syn, and she found herself humming as she turned down a side street.

She felt a sting on her neck and swatted a fly. Her hand came away with blood and she wondered what kind of insect could cause such a bite. She felt a sudden wave of dizziness overtake her and she went to one knee. She had heard of such creatures deep in the wilds, the flying insects that could poison one with a single sting, but she had never heard of one in a city. She went to both knees as her vision swam, then to all fours to try and support herself and stop the world from spinning. She struggled, fighting the darkness that was overtaking her with frightening speed, struggled and then failed as everything went black.

She was in a carriage, it seemed, for even though her eyes were closed she could hear the clop of hoof beats and feel the gentle sway of the coach. Her eyelids were heavy, and she could not seem to get them open, so her hand sought to search about for something familiar. The seat was soft, like velvet, so she thought dreamily it must be a very nice carriage. And she was lying upon something warm, for although there was a chill in the air, she was comfortable, wrapped in something luxurious. Finally, she had enough strength to get the eyelids open, although it took a moment for her blurred vision to focus. And when at last she did focus, it was upon a pair of blue-green eyes that stared down at her with a combination of mild malice, triumph, amusement, but most of all, expectation.

The Lady Jorden leaned down and gently kissed the captive she held in her arms. "Go to sleep," she whispered, and Syn obeyed her.

When she next awoke, Syn was in a far stranger position although extensive lengths had been taken to make her just as comfortable. She was draped over a barrel, her arms and legs bound around the other side. It was hard to tell if it was actually a barrel or a barrel-shaped object, because it was padded and then covered in a soft fur. Whatever it was, Syn felt both vulnerable and ridiculous. Although tightly bound, she was able to turn her head to see that she was naked, her back exposed but with a plush coverlet covering her lower body.

"So, this is where that saying comes from," Syn muttered.

"Over a barrel?" Jorden said, and Syn winced for she had not seen her. "I don't think most of the time it's nearly this comfortable." She walked around to stand in Syn's field of view, patting the padded surface. "I had this specially made for you. I didn't want it too wide or too narrow. It had to be just right."

Syn could feel her heart pound against the padded surface. It slowed slightly when Jorden sat down once more, this time in a position where Syn could see her if she laid her head down sideways. She was dressed in a stunning blue gown that pushed her breasts up and set off her gorgeous eyes. Syn's locket was nestled in the valley between those lovely breasts.

"I have been so patient with you," Jorden said, speaking to her as if she were a wayward child. "I have led you along step-by-step, and yet still you resist. I'm so very tired of waiting."

Jorden lifted an object from the table at her side and Syn's heart started pounding again. It looked like a riding crop. "Do you know what this is?" Jorden asked.

Syn swallowed hard, her focus on the stick. "This is a switch," Jorden said, "one very specially designed. It will not break the skin, in fact, it will not even leave a mark," Jorden said, and her eyes moved to caress the pattern of thin white lines on Syn's back. "It will sting," she continued, "but the pain can be light, really little more than a tingle. Or it can be greater, but it will not cause any damage or permanent harm. The Ha'kan make such wonderful sexual toys," she murmured.

Syn inwardly cursed her newfound friends. What kind of demonic device was this? She half-wondered if they had created the barrel she was strapped onto, but really did not want to know. Her heart started pounding even harder when Jorden again stood.

"So, now we're going to play a little game, you and I," Jorden said, and she trailed the switch along Syn's cheekbone, then down her back. She pulled the coverlet down so she could see Syn's entire body, sighing with pleasure at the sight of the lean torso and long limbs so restrained. She ran the switch across Syn's buttocks then between her legs, causing Syn to jump at the sensation. "Good," she commented, "you have a little movement, that will be important."

"What kind of game?" Syn said, gritting her teeth. She was having a hard time breathing, but it had nothing to do with her position. Then again, it had everything to do with her position.

"You're going to be quiet and still as long as you can," Jorden said, then lightly rapped the switch across her upper back. Syn jumped, but it was more because she was startled than because it hurt. Her heart felt like it was going to burst through her chest wall.

"I moved," Syn said sarcastically, "did that count?"

"That's not the type of movement I'm looking for," Jorden said, and rapped her again. It stung a little, not much more than the tingle Jorden had described. Syn buried her face in the fur.

"What's the matter, my love?" Jorden said wickedly, and then rapped her again, this time a little harder. Syn buried her face in the fur, wishing she could suffocate herself. Jorden traced the switch down her spine, then lightly struck her lower back. Syn again jumped, using the padding and fur to stifle her moan.

"Hmm," Jorden said, "now we're starting to get a little closer." She struck Syn again, only slightly harder than before, and Syn twisted beneath the light blow. Syn muttered something anguished, her face buried in the fur.

"I didn't quite catch that, my love," Jorden said, and struck her again, again eliciting the distressed movement and the muffled imprecation. Syn's entire body was taut and Jorden traced the bunched muscles of her back playfully, then struck her lightly across her lower back again.

Syn moaned into the fur, her agony at a peak. Her nipples were hard, the warm wetness flowed from between her legs, and she could not bear it anymore. She turned her head to the side and whispered something in surrender.

"What was that, my love?" Jorden said, leaning down although she had clearly heard what Syn had said.

"Harder," Syn pleaded, "strike me harder."

And Jorden's pupils widened as she exhaled, at last hearing the submission she craved. She struck Syn, not so hard that it would injure her, but far harder than she had struck her before. And Syn moaned with pleasure, her hips beginning to move against the barrel as she lost both aspects of their game at the same time. And Jorden had to be careful, for she herself was getting lost in the act, and although she was able to moderate the force of the blows, she could not stop from increasing their speed. But it was not fast enough for Syn who writhed beneath the falling switch, utterly relinquishing all control. The restraints tore at her wrists and ankles, doing far more damage than the switch on her back, but that damage was self-inflicted by her own frenzied motion, and in reality, the pain felt just as good. And then Syn released, and released again, and continued to release as she moved against the fur, the restriction in her movement so exciting her it sent her to an entirely new plane of pleasure. She rammed her body against the soft padded surface as the switch fell upon her back until she had nothing left and collapsed on top of the barrel. She could no longer feel her arms or legs and simply hung there limply, nothing more than a beating heart pounding against a chest wall.

Jorden could not catch her breath. She was pressed against Syn's thigh and had literally climaxed right on top of her, although she didn't think Syn had even noticed. She stretched out over the limp form, kissing the back of her neck, her hair, her scars, every inch of that strong back that had yielded to her. She dropped the switch to the ground, forgotten, and undid the restraints that held Syn. Syn would have fallen off the barrel, but Jorden caught her and helped her to the bed. Jorden undid her gown and, wearing only her undergarments, slipped into bed beside Syn, pulling the other woman on top of her and holding her tight. Syn's breathing was still harsh and Jorden could feel her pulse in her chest, and it was a while before both settled to normal. Jorden stroked her hair.

"Why?" Syn said at last.

"Mmm," Jorden said without an iota of repentance, "Because you enjoy that."

Syn turned her head slightly so that she could look up into those blue-green eyes, and Jorden continued. "You want that. And you need it. And I like doing it to you."

"That gives you pleasure?" Syn asked.

"My love, I came right on top of you."

"Oh," Syn said numbly.

Jorden traced her finger along Syn's cheekbone. "You are very possibly the truest submissive I've ever known."

"I am not submissive," Syn said with a vestige of anger, but only a vestige because the words were true.

"Yes," Jorden said, "you are. But there's no shame in that. Unlike others, you don't submit because you're weak, you don't do it for money or personal gain. You care nothing for those things and with your strength you could easily resist me, and yet you do not."

"Why?" Syn asked again.

"Because you don't want to," Jorden said simply.

"You're stronger than you appear," Syn commented.

"And that also excites you."

Syn sighed, and Jorden's hands traced the scars down her back. Jorden knew that these marks played some complicated role in what Syn had become, but things were rarely straightforward. "I won't humiliate you," Jorden said, "ever. I won't degrade you. I don't enjoy those things. But," she said, very matter-of-fact, "I will tie you up and beat you."

Syn did not say anything but did not need to because she was lying on top of Jorden and Jorden could feel her nipples respond. Jorden smiled, but then frowned a little as she took one of Syn's wrists in her hands. There was a red abrasion about it and bruises were already forming.

"This is unacceptable," Jorden said, "I don't want to hurt you. I'll have to devise better restraints."

Syn was dismissive. "I did that to myself, I was so out-of-control."

The thought of Syn's body moving against the barrel in that frenzied motion brought Jorden enormous pleasure. "Ah yes," she said, remembering the picture, "I was thinking perhaps I could mount a phallus-shaped object just below you so that when you moved it would thrust up inside you."

"Oh, dear god," Syn said, not knowing whether to laugh or be horrified. She could actually see what Jorden was describing since the reaction of her body had been so wanton. "Wonderful," Syn said, "then I could fuck myself while you beat me."

"Mmmm," Jorden said, the thought filling her entire body with warmth.

"You are perverse," Syn said with no recrimination.

"I know," Jorden said, still pleasantly imagining the scene. "So, you'll do it?"

"Of course," Syn said, and then went to sleep in her lover's arms.

CHAPTER 13

S yn awoke to find a set of clothing laid out for her. She was not certain where she was, but the furnishings surrounding her told her she was probably in Grenjad once more. She put on the clothes, which were luxurious and fit her perfectly. She pushed through the double doors, wondering if she would be stopped, but there were no guards standing outside. She slowly made her way down the marble staircase, running her hand down the smooth railing. Helga, Jorden's personal servant, was standing at the bottom, but she merely nodded to Syn then continued her task. Syn entered a large living area, one suitable for entertaining guests, and Jorden was sitting there at a desk going over some paperwork. Syn was struck by how different her situation felt. Before, she had been a prisoner, bound and restricted; now she felt like a guest in the manor. She wondered if Jorden would lose interest in her now that she had achieved her goal and so dominated her.

Jorden's blue-green eyes flicked upward. She was pleased to see that Syn was wearing the clothing she had left for her, but she looked so good in it that Jorden considered taking her right back upstairs and taking it off her. There would be plenty of time for that later, she thought. She had relaxed the level of guard within the house but the manor itself was still surrounded. She may have broken her prize down once but there was no guarantee that

Jorden had completely tamed her little thief. That would be a lengthy, albeit enjoyable, process.

"I trust you slept well?"

Syn sat down across from Jorden. The strangeness of the situation was not lost on her, although it appeared to affect the Lady Jorden not at all. Syn was again curious about Jorden's background, how such an intriguing and curious person came into being.

"I slept very well," Syn replied, "and yourself?"

"I slept better than I have in years," Jorden said, and returned to her paperwork.

Syn shifted in her seat. She was about to speak again when Helga walked in.

"My lady?" Helga said, "You have visitors."

Jorden looked up. "I'm not expecting anyone."

"It is the Lord and Lady Maron," Helga said.

"I see," Jorden said icily. "You would think after all these years they would have the grace to give notice."

"Agreed, my lady," Helga said, "would you like me to make arrangements for them to stay in town?"

"That is what I would like," Jorden replied, "but of course not what I will do. Tell them I'm unavailable at the moment and settle them in the guest quarters. I will see to them later."

"As you wish, my lady," Helga said, then departed.

Jorden went back to her paperwork but something in her demeanor had markedly changed. Where before she had been calm and relaxed, Syn noticed that now she seemed on edge, a stiffness to her movements and a distraction in her air. Jorden continued what she was doing for a short while then set it aside. She gazed off at nothing for a moment, then turned her attention to Syn.

"This is comical given that you and I are such a 'non-traditional' couple."

The fact that Jorden described them as a couple inspired a myriad of emotions in Syn, including a small degree of alarm and a much larger degree of pleasure, the latter which made Syn want to slap herself. But she tried to focus on what Jorden was saying as opposed to how she herself was feeling.

"What do you mean?"

"Well, my love," Jorden said, her sarcasm evident, "you get the honor of meeting my parents."

Jorden told Syn she had business to attend to and disappeared. Syn decided to push her new boundaries and she found that although expanded, they were still in place. She was allowed outside, but when she approached the gate, several menacing men moved into her way, so she redirected her path to the courtyard as if that had been her intent all along. Her leash had been lengthened, but she continued to wear the tether about her neck.

Syn moved about the courtyard half-heartedly seeking ways to escape. Really her thoughts were on Jorden's parents and she was greatly curious about them. Curious because of the way Jorden had reacted to their presence, and curious to see if they would provide any insight into the enigma of the noblewoman. So, when Lord Maron came out into the courtyard, Syn did what she was best at and stepped back into the shadows, disappearing.

She examined the man. He was heavyset with a florid complexion, most likely caused by the wine he was swigging even at this early hour. He sprawled onto a bench, his legs wide open, and leered at every servant girl that passed. They all gave him a wide berth save one who either was unfamiliar with him or simply distracted. Either way, she paid for her inattention as he grabbed her breast as she walked past him.

The act shocked Syn. It was not that she was unaware of the liberties noblemen took with their servants. It was because this man was crude, completely at odds with Jorden's cool elegance. His demeanor angered Syn, not only because he was groping the young woman, but because it was an embarrassment and affront to Jorden. It partially explained the coldness of her reception. Syn thought about exiting her hiding place and thrashing the man.

The Lady Maron joined her husband, and Syn noted that her presence did little to diminish the offensiveness of her husband's behavior. Although he did not grope anyone else, he did not hide his admiration for the various body parts of the women he passed, every ogled smirk an insult to his beautiful wife. And she was beautiful, Syn observed. Jorden clearly favored her mother. But the similarities were only superficial as the Lady Maron seemed unwilling or incapable of doing anything about her husband's oafish behavior. She sat quietly, a pained but impotent expression on her face.

Helga entered the courtyard and Syn had the impression she was searching for her. She quietly exited her place of surveillance, careful to make a wide circle around Jorden's parents and approached the maid, who was indeed looking for her. And although Helga had that impassive air that all truly great servants had, Syn could tell she did not much care for Jorden's parents.

Dinner was served early and Syn speculated this was so because the Lord Maron might be too drunk to eat if they waited any longer. Helga had dressed her in very elegant clothing, no doubt picked out by Jorden, and although it fit her as well as the previous outfit, it was a trifle too expensive for her tastes. She felt as if she were going to a costume party, although it was indeed polite of Jorden to give her clothing on par with the occasion.

This made Syn laugh. She had found herself in many ridiculous situations in her lifetime, but this had to the most ridiculous of all. Here she was attending a formal dinner with a woman who was some combination of captor and lover, one so far above her social status that Syn might as well be her slave. And in this strange, quasi-relationship, she was about to meet Jorden's parents, something she had never done with anyone. Certainly, there had been situations where Syn had slept with the daughter and then moved on to the mother, or vice versa, but this was far different. This had more the air of the prospective mate meeting the future in-laws. Syn chastised herself at this train of thought. Jorden had been quite sarcastic about "meeting the parents," so it was obvious it was nothing of the sort.

Still, it was a unique feeling sitting across from Jorden while her parents settled across from one another, and it made Syn wonder for the hundredth time what it must be like to live in such luxury.

"Mother, father, I would like to introduce you to a friend of mine who's visiting from the countryside, Syn."

"That's quite a name," Lord Maron slurred. He glanced dismissively at Syn, for she was not his type. A bit too lanky and not enough breast or backside, plus she was clothed from head-to-toe without a bit of flesh showing. Given enough alcohol, Syn would probably become attractive to him, but he was not there yet.

"I'm very pleased to meet you," Lady Maron said. She was not mousy, merely beaten down, as if a lifetime of slights and insults had removed all life from her. Still, she was gracious and polite, something that could not be said about her husband. From the very first course, Lord Maron began dominating the conversation with his opinions on the empire, the Hyr'rok'kin, local commerce, really anything that he could bluster about in an uninformed manner, and his bluster grew louder with each course as his drink was refilled.

Jorden did not engage much with her father and Syn took her cue from that. It did not seem that Lord Maron wanted anyone else to participate in the conversation, he merely wanted to pontificate. That was fine with Syn. She spent much of the dinner looking from the mother to the father, somewhat baffled by both. This amused Jorden who appeared to take some comfort in Syn's presence and cast her numerous, lingering glances. Syn also took every opportunity to gaze upon Jorden's loveliness, although to Syn's disappointment, she was dressed far more demurely than normal. The Lady Maron was oblivious to all, lost in some private world of her own.

Syn noticed that almost all of the servers were men and judging by what she had seen of Lord Maron's earlier behavior, that was probably by design. When one female servant brought in a side course, Lord Maron undressed her with his eyes in a gross fashion that made his wife sigh aloud and his daughter clench her jaw in icy repose. It disgusted Syn, who was very near going across the table at him. She thought about challenging him to a duel but was not certain of the protocol. She knew that nobility slapped one another with something to initiate the contest, but she figured if she slapped this man as hard as she wanted to, the fight would be over.

It took but one look to ignite that spark to full flame. Jorden's napkin slipped from her lap and she bent to retrieve it. With no attempt at subtlety, Lord Maron leaned forward to leer at his own daughter's breasts. Lady Maron caught the glance and tightened with more emotion than she had displayed since arrival. Syn was far less restrained and leaped to her feet in fury. The guards that watched her every move stepped forward, but escape was not on her mind. She stared at the man, enraged, while he stared at her dumbly from his bleary eyes. She could feel her heart pound against her ribs, and she could feel Jorden's surprised gaze upon her. She wanted to beat this man to death, not only for the look but for what the look implied. Instead, she slammed her chair up against the table, spun about on her heel and stormed from the room. Jorden gave her mother a measured look, then calmly stood and followed Syn.

Syn took the stairs two at a time and slammed into the room that had been her prison. The rage inside her threatened to spill out on everything around her and she wanted to destroy the chairs, the bed, the table, the lamps, everything. She clenched her fists, desperately trying to contain the wrath, but it was overwhelming her. She spun around as Jorden entered their room.

"What's wrong with you?" Jorden asked.

Syn could barely get the words out, so extreme was her anger. "Did he touch you?"

"What?" Jorden asked.

"Did he touch you?" Syn demanded. "Your father! Did he touch you when you were a child?"

Comprehension dawned on Jorden and she let out a great breath. "No."

It was clear that Syn did not believe her, so she elaborated. "He tried, but my mother, who has never been more than a doormat for him to wipe his feet on, for once stood up to him. He beat her almost to death." Jorden's icy composure did not waver although there was an undercurrent of anger in her words.

"I'm going to kill him," Syn announced through clenched teeth.

"No, my love, you're not," Jorden said. Syn's anger was somehow cathartic for her as well.

"Why not?"

Jorden approached her and took Syn's hands in her own. "Because every day that my father lives in my shadow is a punishment worse than death for him. He was but a soldier, and all money and name came from my mother. It didn't take him long to squander both. And now he lives with the reality that I've exceeded him in every way."

"I still don't see why I can't kill him," Syn muttered, although Jorden's words calmed her.

"I don't think I've ever seen this side of you," Jorden said, "this streak of protectiveness. It's really arousing."

Syn's gaze flicked upward, the long eyelashes framing her dark green eyes. Thoughts of Jorden's father drifted away as she looked into those blue-green eyes. Jorden's gaze moved to Syn's lips.

"Perhaps we should do something with all this excess energy you have," Jorden said.

Syn cocked her head to one side. Surely Jorden was teasing her. She could not possibly be suggesting what Syn hoped for, what she longed for. "What did you have in mind?" Syn asked cautiously, unwilling to let her hope run away with her.

"This," Jorden said, and without further hesitation, undid the three buttons that held the top of her gown closed. She parted the cloth and two of the most magnificent breasts that Syn had ever seen spilled out. Syn made a small noise, her hands and lips wanting to move to the lovely peaks, but she would not violate the rules of their game. She licked her lips and tried to find her voice in the throat that had gone dry.

"May I?" she asked.

Jorden smiled with pleasure. "Yes," she said, "you may."

And Syn groaned with the desire that had been pent up while the other released. Her hand went to one breast and her mouth to the other, and so exquisite was the taste and sensation, it might as well have been the first breast she ever kissed. Jorden held Syn's head in her hands, marveling at the skill of that flicking tongue. She had been correct in her assessment of Syn's sexual prowess and was now going to enjoy what she had so long denied herself. She took two steps backward so that her back was against the wall, guiding Syn with her.

"You're going to stand?" Syn murmured, her mouth so busy she could hardly get the words out. "You're far more coordinated than I am."

"I like this position," Jorden said, gazing down at her lover as Syn went to her knees.

"I like it, too," Syn said, trailing her kiss downward, and Jorden's desire flared. The submission in that response was as exciting as that wicked tongue. Syn stopped at the waist where the lower part of the gown was hooked in place. "May I?" Syn asked again, and Jorden caught her breath. "Yes," she said again, "you may."

Syn unhooked the fastenings on the skirt portion and the gown fell to the ground. Jorden wore only her undergarments now, sheer and lacy affairs that Syn thought to add to her current one-piece collection.

"That was a very practiced maneuver," Jorden said chidingly.

"I noticed my clothing has come off effortlessly for you," Syn responded, but before Jorden's anger could flare, added, "But I'm not practicing any-more."

The response soothed and excited Jorden, but she held Syn's head. "Take off your shirt," she said.

Syn complied with the command and pulled her shirt over her head. She then pulled the soft undergarment over her head as well. Jorden could resist running her hands over the thin scars that ran clear up onto her shoulders. Syn was afraid that Jorden would get distracted and not let her finish, but Jorden merely smiled and leaned against the wall. "You may continue," she said.

Syn analyzed their positions. They were about the same height, so even on her knees she was a bit higher than she wished to be. A short footstool caught her eye.

"May I put you on a pedestal?" Syn asked.

Jorden saw her intent. "Yes, you certainly may."

Syn reached for the stool and placed it against the wall, holding Jorden's hand as she stepped up onto the small platform. Now Syn's head was exactly where she wanted it to be. She pulled Jorden's undergarments down to reveal the soft down between Jorden's legs. Syn wanted to go there immediately but restrained herself, stroking the inside of Jorden's thighs and kissing her stomach and the ticklish spot above her hips until Jorden fairly writhed beneath her touch. The fingers would approach the throbbing area but then dance away teasingly until at last Jorden gave her a command.

"You will put your mouth on me now," Jorden ordered through clenched teeth.

"As you wish," Syn said and took her fully in her mouth, suckling and stroking and licking with a passion that had grown for months. Jorden leaned back and looked up at the ceiling, holding Syn's head in her hands as her hips began to move beneath that hungry mouth. And when Syn thrust her fingers up inside of her, she looked down to watch, the sight of that rakish little thief on her knees with her head buried between her legs enough to make her nearly climax on the spot.

But she would not give in that easily, and although Syn's mouth rode her without mercy, Jorden was certain she was bruising that beautiful mouth as she enjoyed the ride. She held Syn's head and when Syn felt Jorden's fingers tangle in her hair, guiding her to press harder, Syn obeyed and brought her to orgasm as the hips rocked back-and-forth beneath her kiss. It seemed to go on forever and brought Syn such pleasure to know that she had at last satisfied the Lady Jorden.

Jorden leaned against the wall, gasping for breath. As much as she loved being in charge, really, the end goal of all that dominance was to completely lose all control. And that was exactly what had happened as her little thief had pushed her to a place she had never been before. She gazed down in disbelief at her flawed, damaged, perfect lover.

"Do you want to remain standing?" Syn said, laughter in her voice. She felt joyful.

"No," Jorden said, mustering her strength, "I think I'll lie down."

Syn fell into the soft covers with Jorden, wrapping her arms about the other woman. Jorden adjusted her so that Syn's head was on her chest, then pulled the blanket over both of them. Normally Syn would have fallen asleep right away. But although she was wonderfully drowsy, sleep did not feel imminent.

"Your body is so perfect," Syn said.

Jorden tilted her head. "You sound surprised."

"No," Syn said, "it's not that. I just, well, you wouldn't show me your body, so I wondered if you were scarred like me."

Jorden squeezed her. "I'm as scarred as you are, my love, mine are just a little less visible."

Syn contemplated these words, and she remembered what had brought them to the room. Evidently, they were both scarred, both from trauma that neither could have avoided nor stopped. It had created a powerful need for control in Jorden and an equally powerful need to be controlled in Syn. Syn had been ashamed of the submissive streak, had hidden it her entire life. It had only been through the playful conversation of Raine and Weynild that she realized, in the right circumstances with the right partner, it could be expressed without fear.

The thought of Raine and Weynild darkened Syn's expression. She still had a job to do, one she was not going to back out of. Fortunately, Jorden was already asleep and therefore could not see the expression of resigned determination on her face.

"Syn!" Skye exclaimed as Raine looked up. "We were all worried about you!"

Syn let her eyes adjust to the dim lighting of the tavern. Raine was seated with her chair against the wall while the Tavinter and the two Ha'kan appeared to be readying their packs. Apparently, she had arrived just in time.

"I was kidnapped again," Syn explained, "although I think the Lady Jorden and I may have come to some sort of understanding."

"I must know everything," Rika said, "what kind of understanding?"

"Well," Syn said uncomfortably, "you know."

"Ah," Rika said, "the kind of understanding that only happens in bed. The best kind," she said with relish.

Raine was curious. "So, after all that, she just let you go?"

Syn looked even more uncomfortable. "Um, no, not exactly. I thought it best just to leave a note."

Skye, Rika, and Dallan all turned to regard her pointedly, and Syn could sense their disapproval from across the room.

"What?" she asked defensively.

"You really don't know anything about women, do you?" Dallan said.

Syn turned to Raine for help, but Raine was shaking her head. "What?" Syn said, holding her hands up in supplication. Raine actually felt sorry for her. It was clear that Syn was in love with this woman.

"Let's put it this way," Raine said, "have you ever left notes like that before?"

Syn blanched. She had left dozens, perhaps even scores.

"And," Raine continued, "did you ever mean any of them or follow up on even one?"

Syn grew paler. Surely Jorden would know that this one was different.

"Did you at least tell her you loved her in the note?" Skye said.

"No," Syn said. She had spent a good ten minutes of internal debate on how to sign the note, and in the end decided against saying "I love you." Jorden had often referred to her as "my love" but she had never actually told

Syn that she loved her, and Syn did not want to be the first to say the words. "No, I didn't," she finished lamely.

"You're an idiot," Rika muttered.

Syn looked stricken and Raine put her arm around her.

"It's all right," she said, "we'll sort it all out when this is through. We'll tell her a dragon threatened you with mortal harm."

Syn nodded, feeling only slightly better. It made her feel ill to think that Jorden would misunderstand her intentions. She wanted only to finish the job, then return to Grenjad. She simply didn't want to take the chance that Jorden would not have let her leave.

The Lady Jorden stood in her chambers staring out the window into the courtyard, and although looking she wasn't seeing anything at all for her thoughts were very distant. Helga stood as far away as she could without leaving the room. She did not think she had ever seen her mistress this angry. And it was a frightening anger, one that alternated between a wintry fury and a seething silence. Helga wanted to say something, anything. She wanted to say that perhaps the note had been legitimate, that the woman had indeed meant what she said. But the Lady's wrath was such that Helga was unwilling to bring it down on herself in defense of that thief.

Jorden could feel the rise and fall of her chest with every fuming breath. She had been a fool to lower her guard with Syn. The woman had finally gotten what she wanted, and no sooner was the deed done than she was gone before morning. Jorden crumpled the note in her hand into a ball. How many notes had Syn left exactly like this one? She probably laughed as she signed her name and slipped out the window. The time for games was over. She was going after her prey for real now.

"Helga?"

"Yes, my lady?"

"Bring me my armor."

The very act of saying the words brought Jorden pleasure. She began wiping the makeup from her face, and then splashed cold water from the basin.

This time, she thought, this time she just might kill that thief.

CHAPTER 14

Syn was in awe of her companions. Raine moved through the forest without fear, loping along as if she were a wild animal. The two Ha'kan had transitioned from playful, light-hearted individuals into two of the most fearsome warriors Syn had ever seen, a magnificent sight in their polished leather armor, bristling with weapons.

And the Tavinter was a wonder beyond that. If Raine was at home in the forest, then Skye was a part of it. She could see and smell things that no one else was even aware of. She could read the tracks on the ground as if they were telling a story. And she plucked things here-and-there from the trees and bushes, munching on berries and nuts. When she saw Syn's interest, she began explaining the various plants and mushrooms as she went along, and Syn was amazed at the breadth of her knowledge. It did not seem there was any plant or animal that Skye did not know.

It was a testament to Raine's senses, then, that she and Skye sensed danger at the same time, and both stopped abruptly. Skye crouched down instinctively and Syn followed. Raine, on the other hand, froze in place as if a statue, her hand poised above her sword, and the two Ha'kan followed her lead. None of the five moved. Syn looked to Skye, then to Raine. Skye sniffed the air, peering through the forest around them. Raine seemed perfectly relaxed, motionless but with little alarm.

"How many of them?" Raine whispered to Skye.

"Not a large group," Skye whispered back, "not even a dozen."

Raine grinned. "Good, just enough to loosen my sword arm."

"Not a dozen what?" Syn whispered to Rika, who was closest to her.

"Hyr'rok'kin," Rika answered.

Syn stood upright and would have bolted into the forest if Rika had not grabbed her and lifted her from her feet. It was a ridiculous response born of sheer terror, perhaps the worst possible option Syn could have chosen, but instinct had bred only two reactions in her. She was not much of a fighter so she could only flee, and that had been her impulse. Fortunately, Rika was strong enough to subdue her with little effort.

"Shh!" Rika said, holding her tightly.

But there was already a rustling in the forest ahead of them, and Raine sighed.

"I was going to sneak up on them, but I guess a frontal assault is just as good."

And then Raine was gone, and the four of them followed with Rika practically carrying Syn. They were not moving with any particular haste, and as frightened as she was, Syn wondered why they were not rushing to assist Raine. When they arrived in the opening in the trees, Syn realized it was because Raine did not need any assistance.

The blue-eyed warrior did not have one sword arm but two that dealt death with equal efficiency. She was surrounded by hideous, blackened, pig-like creatures that squealed and roared in pain and anger. The monstrosities looked like animals but wore blood-encrusted armor and wielded swords and axes that were equally as filthy. Foam spewed from hairy muzzles as saliva dripped from razor-sharp teeth as the Shards sought to overwhelm Raine.

And suddenly, Syn was eight years old again. She was watching in horror as her parents were set upon by the foul creatures. She could hear the snap of her mother's neck that proved merciful as she went down under the swarming horde. And she could hear the screams of her father as he was far less mercifully devoured alive. And Syn turned and ran, crashing through the hated forest, running for her very life. Her lungs burned, her eyes were hot with tears, her throat felt on fire, but still she ran and she ran and she ran, just as she had been running every day of her life since. She felt shame and bitterness over her inability to help her parents, shame over her cowardice and fear, shame that she lived while her parents died so horribly.

"Hey!" Rika said, gently shaking her. At first Rika had thought Syn a weakling to react in such a way, but it was apparent there was more to Syn's response than mere cowardice. "Look, Raine is fine."

And Raine was fine, and in fact more than fine as she laughed and danced about, slicing the creatures in two with glorious skill. She impaled one, decapitated another, amputated the legs of a third, and finally sliced the throat of the last one standing. The carcasses lay strewn about the meadow, twitching in the thick, humid air, and all was silent once more. Raine wiped her swords on the cloth sleeve of one dead Shard, then casually returned the weapons to the crossed sheaths on her back. She wore the grin that had been on her face throughout the battle.

"No Marrow Shard," she commented, "how disappointing."

"You're the only person I know who wishes for those creatures," Skye said.

Raine approached Syn, noting her pallor. "Are you all right?"

Flies were already gathering on the corpses and Syn viewed the carnage with a haunted look in her eyes. Rika released her and Syn took a deep breath.

"My parents were slaughtered by Hyr'rok'kin when I was eight years old," Syn said, "right in front of me. Or at least right in front of me until I ran away."

"I'm sorry," Raine said, regretting her joking comment about the Marrow Shard. "I didn't know."

"It's not your fault. I don't talk much about it. And I'm sorry I jumped and gave away our position."

"'Tis no concern," Skye said. "And you're never in danger from the Hyr'rok'kin if Raine is around."

"I like to kill them," Raine said, a gleam in her eye.

"I can see that," Syn said, looking over the meadow piled high with bodies. Dallan patted her on the shoulder.

"The first time we met Raine she saved us from the Shards. We were on a field exercise while still at the Academy and were set upon by a small army of Hyr'rok'kin. We killed three, maybe four of them then Raine showed up and killed fifty or sixty of them, including a Marrow Shard."

"Then the dragon showed up and killed even more," Rika added. "Then the dragon transformed and embarrassed Dallan, which was the best part of all."

Dallan turned red at the memory while Skye laughed out loud. Syn felt the warmth of friendship from the women, and she was amazed at their irrepressible humor. For the first time in a very long time, she felt safe, which was odd since she was getting ready to embark on one of the most dangerous jobs in her career.

"Come along," Raine said, wrinkling her nose, "the stench will be bad before too long."

The band had traveled an additional half a day when Skye and Raine again sensed something simultaneously. Skye smelled the smoke from the distant campfire and Raine paused, also sniffing the breeze. There was a hint of mint, some spices, and a few more noxious odors that indicated alchemy or perhaps the mixing of potions. Raine tilted her head to one side, assessing the combination of smells.

"Do you know what that is?" Skye asked.

"Yes, I do," Raine replied. "It's not dangerous. Well, it is dangerous," she corrected, "just not to us. I'm surprised they're here, though. They usually stay closer to the Wilds."

Raine pushed through the trees, followed by Skye, who was followed by Dallan. Syn was comfortably sandwiched between the two Ha'kan as Rika brought up the rear. They came through an opening in the trees into a small meadow.

"Oh, witches," Skye murmured. There were many witches in the forests of her land and the Tavinter often traded meat and hides for potions, or even better, the recipes for the potions. Witches could be unpredictable, but as long as they were treated fairly and with respect, they were harmless.

Well, perhaps harmless wasn't the appropriate word. The beautiful witch with the striking light green eyes gave Raine an incendiary look that would have melted a lesser being. Skye wondered if Raine ever got used to people looking at her that way.

"Hello Valka, Unna," Raine said, nodding to the second witch who came out from the tent flap.

"Raine," the green-eyed witch said, acknowledging her, and Unna smiled brightly and merely nodded. Valka approached Raine, lifted her hand, then stroked Raine's cheek. There was an inadvertent flash of violet in Raine's eyes at the sensual contact, and her hand flashed upward, grasping Valka's wrist. The Scinterian markings on her forearm were visible in bold relief, but Valka just smiled at the threat and danger they implied.

"I merely toy with you, Raine, you know I would not defy Talan." Valka's gaze took in the whole of Raine's lithe frame before returning to linger on her lips. "Although it might be worth it. I know no spell would work on you, but there are a few potions I would love to try." She turned her attention to the group as a whole. "You travel with some interesting companions." She assessed Skye. "A Tavinter," her eyes moved to Dallan and Rika, "two Ha'kan," her eyes settled on Syn, who was unsuccessfully attempting to hide behind Rika, "and a thief," she finished, biting off the last word.

"Oh, that's right," Raine said, turning to Syn, "you've already met the Raven sisters."

Syn cleared her throat. "Yes, yes, we've met."

"And you agreed to pay a toll were we ever to cross paths again," Valka said with a trace of malicious humor.

Syn's discomfiture told Raine all she needed to know. "Trading in your usual currency?" she said with a laugh.

"You know 'tis all I have," Syn mumbled.

"Hmm. I cannot help you pay that toll," Raine said, "so you're on your own."

Rika elbowed Syn while Raine continued her conversation with Valka. "What currency is that?" she whispered.

"Sexual favors," Syn whispered back angrily, "what do you think?"

"Perhaps I could help you with that debt," Rika murmured, examining the attractive witch with the light-green eyes.

"You're insane," Syn whispered.

"I like to think of it as adventurous," Rika whispered back.

"There's something I would ask of you," Valka said, speaking to Raine, and although the timbre of her voice hardly changed, Raine recognized the shift to a more serious topic.

"Very well," she said formally, "although we're currently on a quest of some importance."

"This would take you no more than a day," Valka said, "and I would be greatly in your debt."

"All right," Raine said, "let us discuss it over dinner. I'm sure my companions are hungry."

Syn and Skye went to a nearby stream and caught enough fish for a hearty meal. Unna set about preparations, wrapping the fish in broad, flat leaves filled with spices, mushrooms, and tender roots. The witches served their guests a veritable feast, one Dallan thought rivaled the fare of the Ha'kan royal kitchen. They sat about the fire on logs, laughing and eating their fill. Unna then brought out a pungent, mint liqueur, one gratefully sipped by the drowsy group as they settled in for the night. Only Raine seemed immune to fatigue, sitting quietly as she gazed into the fire.

"So, why don't you tell me what it is you want me to do?"

Valka turned her light green eyes onto the Scinterian. "It's a trivial task," she said, "one that's hardly a challenge for someone like you."

Raine said nothing.

"There were some poachers, in our forest near the Wilds, and they took some game."

"And?" Raine prompted. Poachers were a problem, but many were hunting simply to feed their families. And although the Raven sisters claimed a large part of the forest as their territory, that claim was based more on the fear they instilled rather than any valid contract.

"And I wish you to track them down."

Raine examined her closely. "I'll not kill some poachers because they trespassed on your land."

"That's not what I wish. They took a—"

Valka paused, then cleared her throat. "They took a doe, killed her. I merely wish the hide back, the antlers, whatever is left."

Raine continued to assess Valka. "Very well. And why do you not do this yourself?"

"We followed the hunters to the red trees, which is why we're here so far from the Wilds. But the red trees create a miasmic eddy."

"I see," Raine said. Just as there were places in Arianthem where magic was plentiful, there were places where it was absent or unpredictable. A miasmic eddy was one such confluence, a void where magic often did not work or went awry. As powerful as Valka was, she could be rendered impotent in such a place. "I think I understand," Raine said, saying much by saying little. "How many hunters?"

"I believe there were four, no more."

"I'll take Skye with me early in the morning, if you would be so kind as to entertain my Ha'kan friends and my thief for a day."

Raine had to convince Dallan and Rika that they were off on a trivial task because neither wished Skye to go without them. But it was not the triviality of the task that swayed them; it was the fact that she would be with Raine, and therefore protected beyond measure. So, Dallan and Rika contented themselves with spending the day talking with Valka and Unna, women who fascinated them because they had never met witches before. There were few within Ha'kan territories, and although there were many in the Tavinter forests when they had been on campaign, they tended to avoid the heavily armed Ha'kan forces. Syn sat off by herself, trying to avoid eye contact with the two witches, especially the light green eyes that swiveled her way, entertained by her situation and discomfort.

Raine and Skye made very quick progress through the forest, and it was not long before Skye picked up the trail of the band Valka had described. But as she kneeled down to examine the markings that told her a complete story, she had a bemused look on her face.

"What's wrong?"

Skye trailed her finger through the dirt. "Well, there are four of them like Valka said, three men and a woman. And they have one horse, old, partially lame, and very heavy-laden."

"What else?"

"They have several wounded animals with them."

Raine furrowed her brow. "Why would they do that?"

A scowl crossed over Skye's fine features. "I've seen this before. I expelled these type of poachers from my own forests. They're too lazy to cleanly kill the animals and cure the meat properly, so they keep them alive, in agony, so that the meat stays fresh. It's a horrible practice. The animals are in constant pain. They trap them, then cut their tendons or break a leg so they can't run, then drag them along behind them. And it serves no purpose because the meat is no good by the time they kill the animal."

Skye stood upright once more. "My people hunt for food, hunt to survive, but we don't kill for sport and we don't want to cause pain. This disgusts me."

But that meant that the doe might still be alive, Raine thought. "We have to move faster."

Although Raine could have easily tracked the poachers, she was glad that Skye was with her. Skye's vision was so keen that she could follow the trail almost at full speed, and the two ran through the forest. It was not long before the leaves on the trees took on a reddish hue, and Raine knew they were nearing their destination. Voices drifted toward them and both slowed abruptly. Raine took the lead as the two silently moved forward.

They peered through the underbrush and Raine saw that once again, Skye's tracking abilities were unmatched. Three men and a woman sat around a fire. A pitiful looking horse stood off to the side, mange covering his ill-kempt coat. A make-shift pen was sloppily built on the other side, although Raine saw no purpose in the pen as the animals within barely moved. A young wolf lay on his side, his hind legs crushed so that he dragged himself about by his forelegs. A doe lay near him, also lamed, and it was a testament to her misery she demonstrated no fear from her mortal enemy, the wolf. A crow sat perched on the top rail of the pen, his wing hanging limp and broken, and one foot pulled up into his side as if injured.

Skye pulled her bow from her back. "I'm going to put those animals out of their misery."

"No," Raine said quietly but urgently. "We can't do that."

Skye was surprised. As deadly as Raine was, she was not cruel. But Skye realized she did not completely understand the situation because Raine was clearly seething, just unwilling to move. One of the hunters walked too near the young wolf and the canine gave a pathetic, instinctive snap towards him. The hunter laughed and kicked at the young wolf.

"Well," Raine said, "now we need do nothing because they just sealed their fate."

A single, mournful howl drifted through the forest. All four poachers whirled towards the eerie sound. One laughed nervously and made a rude remark, and the others tried to laugh it off as well. But a second, mournful howl, this one from the opposite direction, cut short their forced mirth.

Skye glanced back. This one had come from behind them. She felt Raine's hand on her arm.

"Don't be afraid. We're surrounded, but we're not in any danger. They, however," she said, nodding somberly towards the poachers, "are all dead."

Even with her astonishing hearing, Skye could barely hear the padded footsteps as they crept through the forest. She tried to count their number, thinking at first it was dozens, then realizing it was scores. The howls continued, the unnerving chorus growing in volume as more and more voices joined in. The poachers moved to the center of the clearing near the fire, pressing against each other fearfully. The first wolf came into the open and the nearest hunter raised his bow as if to fire, but another wolf appeared to his right, snapping at him. His bow wavered between the two targets, uncertain which to take down, but a third, then a fourth appeared, so he stayed his hand, overwhelmed. Another poacher had drawn a dagger, but it, too, wavered indecisively due to the sheer number of potential attackers.

The circle of wolves closing in on the poachers stunned Skye. The Tavinter did not hunt wolves. The meat was not good, and they would not kill for the hides alone. And contrary to the popular myths about the predators, Skye knew wolves were fearful of people and rarely attacked unless provoked or cornered. So, the fact that this army was closing in on the hunters was shocking and unnatural.

And then the hunter with the bow made a terrible mistake. His fear overcame him and he loosed an arrow at the nearest wolf. It did not land, however, as something enormous leaped into the clearing and with a colossal paw, swiped the arrow from the air into the ground. The poachers screamed and fell to their knees, while to Skye's stunned gaze, the gigantic wolf stood up on two legs, towering over the small band. A roar shook the forest that caused a flurry of leaves to fall to the ground. The enormous wolf raised a giant paw, the sharp claws gleaming in the dim light, prepared to strike.

"Wait, wait," Raine said, rising to her feet and brushing leaves from her armor. Skye was stunned to see her casually walk into the middle of the impending carnage. She was even more astonished to see the giant wolf, pause, turn towards her with a baleful yellow-eyed stare, then speak to her.

"I knew you were going to do that."

The wolf's voice was low and rolled out like thunder. His tone was slightly sarcastic but also filled with affection. The fact that the monster spoke, however, was enough for the poacher with the bow and he sprang to his feet and ran towards Raine in a complete panic.

"By the gods!" he screamed. "Please help us! By all that is sacred, plea—"

Raine hit him hard, squarely on the jaw, so fierce a blow it not only stopped him but knocked him backward to where he started his flight. He went down in a crumpled heap.

"Thank you," Fenrir said, slightly mollified. "I feel better."

"Me, too," Raine said, then turned her wrath on the cowering poachers. "You are in the presence of a god," she said through clenched teeth, "and you will stay on your knees."

Skye had started to get to her feet but Raine's words stopped her and she went back to the ground. "Not you," Raine said, rolling her eyes. Skye again slowly got to her feet, stepping with wonder through the throng of wolves, all who had calmed instantly at Raine's first words and who now sat placidly on their hindquarters. The great wolf eyed her for a moment, then directed his attention to Raine, who was glaring at the poachers in disgust.

"Fenrir, these people are ignorant and stupid. Surely, you'll not slaughter them because they lack the wisdom and civility of your kind."

Fenrir sighed. "I knew you were going to appeal to my better side. What would you have me do?"

"Obviously, you may do as you will. But I suggest that these four serve you and your kind for the rest of their lives." She gave a kick at the nearest one, who cowered at the slight nudge. "How does that sound?"

"Yes, yes," the poacher sobbed. "We'll do anything. We'll never hunt again! Anything his lordship wishes!"

"They aren't much as subjects," Raine muttered, "and you feel free to kill them if they go back on their word."

This brought about many protestations of loyalty from the cringing group. "Just shut up," Raine said. She moved to the injured wolf, gently picking him up from the pen. He whimpered slightly from pain, and Raine buried her head in his mane. She carried him to the giant wolf, who went to all fours so she, on tiptoe, could place the wounded creature on his back.

"I'll take care of my pup," Fenrir rumbled. "But I cannot help that one."

"I know," Raine said of the doe. "I'll carry her away."

Raine leaned forward and buried her head in the monster's mane while Skye stared in wonder. Then, the great wolf and the Scinterian bowed to one another, and the pack and their god disappeared silently into the forest. One young wolf stayed behind, bouncing about with his tail wagging, but Raine shook her head.

"I'll play with you later," she admonished, "you'll scare the doe."

To Skye's astonishment, the wolf seemed to understand, even to have a look of disappointment on his canine features as he barked once, then disappeared after the rest of his pack. She watched his departure dumbly.

"Are you okay?" Raine asked.

"Um, yes," Skye replied. Her companion was the sole survivor of two mythic races and the mate of a dragon, so she was not certain why any of this even surprised her.

"Good," Raine said. She gave another kick at the cowering poachers. "You've sworn your loyalty to Fenrir, and I assure you he will destroy you if you go back on your word. Now get out of my sight."

The four scrambled to their feet and fled through the forest, leaving everything behind. Raine removed the saddle and trappings from the decrepit horse. "I don't know how you'll do, old fellow, but at least you're free now."

The horse snorted, pawed at the ground with a hoof, then trotted off into the forest. Raine approached the black bird. "Hmm," she said, "that's appropriate. This isn't a crow but a raven. Perhaps you can give this fellow a ride?"

The bird was very calm as Raine lifted it gently. It balanced on its one good foot, and Skye placed it on her gauntlet, tucked up against her body so it did not have to worry about falling. "But what about her?" Skye asked.

Raine kneeled down and placed a hand on the agonized doe, trying to soothe it. "I'm going to have to carry her."

Skye knew that Raine was immensely strong, but they had come a vast distance through the forest. "I can help you."

"No," Raine said, and with one smooth move, lifted the doe onto her shoulders, draping it around her neck as gently as possible. "I have her."

It took them much longer to return and the sun was setting by the time they neared the witch's camp. Raine had never once stopped for rest or even slowed her pace, carrying her great burden. It was only her concern for the doe's injuries that kept them at a more sedate pace, otherwise Skye was certain Raine could have run with that animal upon her back.

Their appearance was greeted with a flurry of activity. Dallan and Rika had begun to grow concerned at their extended absence and greeted them joyfully. But it was Valka and Unna who rushed forward, stunned at the sight of Raine carrying the deer upon her back.

"She lives?" Valka said in disbelief, emotion thickening her voice.

"Barely," Raine said, her tone grim, "but yes, she lives."

Raine sat the doe down ever so gently on a blanket next to the fire. Unna rushed over, poultices in hand, tears on her cheeks. Valka kneeled down, and it was the oddest sight to see the fearsome witch cradle the wounded animal in her arms. Raine stepped backward while her companions looked on the strange scene with curiosity.

"Raine," Skye said, noticing for the first time that the doe had the oddest light green eyes. "Why couldn't Fenrir help the doe?"

Raine's tone was tinged with sadness. "Because only the one who cursed her could remove that curse."

Valka spoke words in a commanding, guttural tone and the ensuing flash of light caused Rika to reach for her sword. Raine's hand on her arm stayed her action.

"It's all right," Raine said.

The doe cried out once, then twisted and transformed into a young woman, a young woman who bore a remarkable resemblance to Valka.

"Mother," the girl sobbed, "I'm so sorry I disobeyed you."

Valka struggled with her own emotion. "No, I'm sorry. I meant only to punish you, not to harm you."

Unna leaned down and hugged her niece, offering her cool water which the girl gratefully took. Skye had tears in her eyes and even Syn, as incorrigible a scoundrel as she was, had a lump in her throat.

"Valka," Raine said, "I know Unna is a very talented alchemist and can mix potions, but there are wood elves, the Halvor, near here, several who are powerful healers."

Valka could not look away from her daughter, whose own eyes drifted closed with exhaustion. Unna was pleased to see the mild sedative she had given her already taking hold.

"I know the elves you speak of, but they don't care for outsiders."

"That won't be a problem," Raine said. She pivoted, and in the view of her companions, began to address the empty forest.

"You can come out now."

A very sheepish wolf crept out from the underbrush, and Skye recognized the youngster that had stayed behind before, the one that wished to play with Raine.

"Did you think I couldn't hear you trampling around behind us?" Raine said, scolding. "I thought it was some stupendous pig making its way through the forest!"

The wolf hung its head in shame, eliciting smiles of wonder from Raine's companions. "All right," Raine said, relenting, "perhaps not a pig. But you need to work on that."

The young wolf still looked embarrassed, so Skye whispered to him. "I didn't hear you."

The pup yelped in happiness, then settled onto his hindquarters awaiting instruction.

"I need you to find Elyara," Raine said. "You know where she is?"

The wolf again yelped in response.

"Good, find her and bring her here."

The wolf leaped to his feet, did one quick circle wagging his tail, then bounded off into the forest. Raine watched him go, and finally allowed the tension to drain from her body. "I'm tired," she said to all present, "and I think I'm going to sleep. We can leave in the morning."

Unna escorted her inside the tent to her own bedroll, indicating that Raine should sleep in the warm furs. Under normal circumstances, Raine would have declined and slept on the ground, but she sensed Unna's immense gratitude was seeking an outlet, so she acquiesced gracefully and was asleep within minutes.

Outside, Rika offered her assistance and gently lifted Valka's daughter into her arms, following Valka into the tent. When Rika came back out, Dallan released the breath she had been unconsciously holding for an extremely long interval.

"Skye!" she exclaimed, "Tell us what happened! What a magical adventure!"

131

"You can't even imagine," Skye said in wonder, "and I tell you this: I will never look at a wolf the same way again."

In the morning, Raine awoke early. She was relieved that Valka's daughter, although no better, was at least no worse and had survived the night.

"She wouldn't have lasted another day," Valka said to her. "I am eternally grateful to you."

Raine flashed her brilliant smile. "You're welcome, and Elyara should be here within a day."

"I can never thank you for what you've done."

"Well," Raine said, glancing over at Syn, "there is the matter of my thief's toll. I believe she's fallen for some noblewoman, so I don't think she can fulfill her duty. Her days of debauchery may be coming to an end."

"I find that difficult to believe," the beautiful witch said drily. "But you have more than paid her toll."

Just then, the raven, his wing bound and with a little bandage on his foot, croaked loudly. He was happy, hopping about on the stand that Unna had built for him and placed near the fire so he would be warm.

"Then we bid you farewell," Raine said.

"Safe travels," Valka replied.

CHAPTER 15

Once moving again, they made good time. They were about halfway to their destination, Raine judged, because they were nearing the only major thoroughfare through this part of the country. The roadway cut through the center of the forest from north to south and was not well-maintained for political reasons. To the north was the Alfar Republic, the high elves that lived in the mountains. The Alfar would engage in commerce with the dwarves and sons and daughters of men, however they held almost all cultures as inferior to their own. They especially looked upon the Empire with disdain, thinking them upstarts compared to their ancient culture. They were slightly more favorably inclined toward the Ha'kan, but even then, their arrogance was grating upon the elegant women of the all-female race.

It was one of the great disputes between the Alfar and the Empire that the elves were allowed complete access to imperial lands whereas Alfar territory was largely off limits. The Alfar were very particular who was granted entry to their country and ingress was greatly restricted. Because of this, almost all barter and trade took place within imperial cities. Travel on this roadway, therefore, was almost always Alfar merchants, either bringing goods to the cities or returning home with gold. The Emperor had sought on several occasions to change this dynamic through treaties, tariffs, or trade agreements, but the sad fact was that there was little the Alfar wanted or needed from the imperials, whereas there was much the Alfar possessed that the imperials greatly desired. The only thing the Emperor could do in response was fail to maintain the roadway, which did little more than irritate the Alfar merchants and make them drive up their prices.

Raine had traveled this road many times before. Rough as it was, it was an easier route than through the forest, but it would have added days to their journey. She knew they would cross it at some point and assumed they would see no one upon the thoroughfare, which is why she stopped short when they reached the overhang that looked down upon the roadway.

"Is that an army?" Dallan asked uncertainly.

Alfar troops marched eight abreast across the roadway for as far as the eye could see in either direction. The military cohorts were broken up by regiments on horseback, and mixed amongst both types of troops were elaborate carriages. Raine had seen Alfar merchant caravans that were always heavily guarded, but this was something different.

"No," she replied, "these are Alfar, which means that everything is a procession." She examined the size of the parade. "Even so, this is someone important." She turned to Dallan. "Will they recognize you?"

Dallan shook her head. "The Alfar and the Ha'kan have diplomatic relations and they maintain an embassy in our capital. Still, it's unlikely they would know me."

"Hmm," Raine said, "but you look more like your mother each day. I want you to remain hooded. And you as well," she said, nodding to Rika.

Although mesmerized by the pageantry of the advancing Alfar, this snippet of conversation attracted Syn's attention, and she again wondered at the identities of her companions. Raine's next comment furthered her curiosity as Raine turned to Skye.

"And you?" she asked.

"The Tavinter and Alfar have no formal relationship, but we get along with them better than most. Even so, the Tavinter pride themselves on being unseen, and I doubt they would have even recognized my father although he dealt with them for years."

"Good," Raine said. She pulled her own hood up. "Then let's head down and see if we can get across."

The four followed Raine down the hill and hung back when she motioned for them to slow. She approached the procession and her presence attracted the attention of several of the mounted cavalry. Their gleaming helmets swiveled about as they looked arrogantly down at her.

"You there, you will halt."

"This is an imperial highway," Raine said, "I will go where I will."

Three of the elven warriors drew their swords and a ripple of conversation traveled down the procession.

"I suggest you put those swords away," Raine said mildly.

"Or what?" the nearest soldier said with contempt.

Raine lowered her hood. Before she had spoken in the common language, but now she spoke flawless elvish. "Or I will take them from you."

The skilled use of their language was startling, and her appearance caused another ripple down the procession. This time the progression slowed, then stopped. The warriors stared down at the stunning young woman. She appeared human but obviously was not. She had an air of lethal composure that made them uneasy. Skye watched the interaction, curious. Raine was normally not so confrontational and although Skye could not understand the elvish language, Raine seemed to be deliberately provoking them.

A female captain rode forward. "You would interfere with a diplomatic mission?" she demanded.

Raine cocked her head to the side. She had successfully elicited the information she sought, but now that brought about more questions.

"A diplomatic mission?" Raine asked. "From the Alfar?"

The Alfar Ambassador peered out from the concealment of her carriage. She had felt the procession lurch to a stop, and it caused a swell of irritation. But now she was curious about the creature who had so boldly walked up and stopped a small army. She was not certain if the woman was brave, impudent, or simply insane. Normally premeditation ruled her decision-making and therefore her aide was slow to respond when she motioned she wished to exit. He recovered, however, and opened the door. He stepped out and then with prodigious formality assisted her from the carriage. This caused considerable consternation amongst the troops and the horses danced about, sensing their riders' unease.

Raine stared at the elven female. She possessed the refined beauty of all the Alfar, the sharp, aristocratic features, the almond-shaped eyes, the curve of the ears to a point. Her eyes were a light brown, almost gold color and her hair was fashioned in an elaborate, intricate braid that went to her waist. She was tall and willowy, slender like all the high elves, and Raine thought she was exceptionally lovely even for an Alfar. But it was not her exquisite good looks that occupied Raine's attention, but rather that she looked very familiar.

Maeva in turn examined Raine. This one could not possibly be human and must have Alfar blood in her veins because surely Sjöfn herself had fashioned such a face and body. Although Maeva preferred her conquests young and small, petite even, the creature before her was the embodiment of perfection. And although the woman was far from Maeva's preferred archetype, she felt a startling surge of desire, almost lust, that was unnerving.

The silence between the two lengthened, and it was Raine who finally broke it.

"You are the Alfar Ambassador?"

"Yes," the elf said coolly, "my name is Maeva."

Raine had hoped a name might solve the mystery of why the woman looked familiar, but it helped not a bit.

"And where is your diplomatic mission headed?"

"I don't see how that's any of your business," Maeva said with slight condescension. Her perusal covered the length of Raine's frame. "But I will humor you. We are on our way to the imperial capital."

"The Empire?" Raine said, "That's surprising."

None of the Alfar troops had any idea why the Ambassador was engaging this perfect stranger in conversation, and Maeva herself was not certain why she was divulging such information.

"Have the Hyr'rok'kin been in your lands?" Raine asked with concern. It was the only thing she could think of that would elicit such an astonishing response from the Alfar.

Maeva's eyes narrowed. This woman was remarkably prescient and spoke with a calm authority that made her wonder who she was.

"Not yet," Maeva replied. "And many among the Alfar think that it won't happen, that the Empire should deal with the menace on their own. But my brother, whose council I accept unequivocally, believes it's time to foster new alliances."

"Your brother is very wise."

"There are very few who have actually been through the Veil to the gates of the Underworld," Maeva said, "so if he speaks of the threat of the Hyr'rok'kin, I listen."

Understanding dawned on Raine, and the nagging sense of familiarity dissolved into pleased recognition.

"Feyden," she said, "your brother is Feyden."

Maeva was stunned. There was no way this person could know that. Her eyes drifted down to the weapons the woman carried, the double swords, the long sword, a strange-looking device that appeared to be a folded bow. Her survey moved back to the ethereal beauty of that face.

"You are Raine," she murmured

"Yes," Raine said, "Feyden is a dear friend of mine."

And Maeva understood. This was the dragon slayer and the dragon's lover, the half-Scinterian, half-Arlanian that her brother admired more than any other being in the world. Feyden said little publicly of his adventures but Maeva was his twin and he had shared all with her. Although she and Feyden were utterly reserved, she had subtly teased him about his infatuation with the woman. Now that she knew the woman's identity, Maeva was relieved about her surge of unexplained lust. The Alfar had long worshipped the Arlanians before the race went extinct, valuing the gifts of their trysts more than any silver or gold.

"Then it's fate that we should meet in such a way. I'm not optimistic of any developments from my work. I personally hold nothing but disdain for the imperials, but it's Feyden's belief such an alliance is necessary."

Such an alliance was crucial, Raine thought, if Weynild's foresight was correct.

"I have a few matters to take care of, but I would be happy to assist in any way needed," Raine said formally.

"We'll be holding talks with the imperials, the Dverger, and the Ha'kan over the next few months," Maeva said. One of Raine's hooded companions shifted, catching Maeva's attention, but then she returned her cool gaze to Raine. "I expect the talks with the Dverger to be the most productive as we share a common lineage, and then I'll move on to the respective capitals."

"I'll follow your progress and make myself available."

"Thank you," Maeva said. She nodded to the elven captain. "Make a path for her and her companions to pass."

The cohort parted with military precision and the five were able to cross the road. Maeva took that opportunity to examine the figures with Raine. Two were quite large and hooded, one was an unremarkable human, and one was a fair-haired, hazel-eyed beauty with an almost elven complexion. She was much closer to Maeva's type, although a little tall for her liking. Maeva returned her attention to the Arlanian. She liked slender elven males or petite little females, but she would bed the Arlanian without hesitation. Raine gave her a brilliant smile in parting and Maeva fully understood Feyden's crush.

She re-entered her carriage, and the procession continued while the Ambassador mused for hours on this strange quirk of fate.

CHAPTER 16

They made remarkable time from then on and now stood before a placid lake that was deceptively picturesque. "I will stop here," Raine announced, gazing out over the blue water. A round stone structure was on the far side. "Can you get Syn to the tower?" she asked, turning to Skye.

Skye crouched down and began examining the terrain with a practiced eye. One side of the lake looked to be far easier going, but the other side would offer far more concealment. It would take longer, but it would be the safer of the two routes.

"Yes," she said, "we'll go that way."

Raine nodded. "Good. I cannot go further with you." She moved to Skye and put her hands on her shoulders. "Are you sure you're up to facing Ingrid? It's my hope you won't have to, that you'll get in and out undetected, but are you prepared just in case?"

Syn noticed that Skye grew pale at the mention of the sorceress. It seemed she was not the only one facing down demons on this quest.

"Yes," Skye said, "I'm prepared."

"I promise that I'll be there if you need me," Raine said, then directed her comment to Syn. "And that goes for you, too."

The two young women nodded, and Skye started off into the forest with Syn behind. Dallan and Rika started to follow.

"And where do you think you two are going?" Raine asked.

"We're not letting her go by herself," Dallan said.

"You're going to have to," Raine insisted. "I chose these two because of their stealth, and none of us can match that. If I thought I could, I would go myself."

"I don't like this," Dallan said, her jaw clenching.

"Nor I," Rika agreed.

"You're going to have to trust me," Raine insisted.

Both wore dark looks on their faces, but relented. Syn watched, puzzled, as Skye kissed Dallan goodbye passionately, then turned and kissed Rika with the same passion. She made a note to herself that, if she survived this job, she was going to have to ask the Ha'kan about their sexual habits because her curiosity was killing her. Skye started off into the forest and Syn followed.

"I don't like this," Dallan repeated, watching the two disappear. "What if the sorceress can sense Skye?"

"She may already have," Raine murmured, staring across the lake at the distant tower.

"What?" Dallan said.

"Calm yourself," Raine said. "I don't know for certain that she can. But it was one of the reasons why I couldn't accompany them."

"You would send them into a trap?" Rika said, her tone accusing.

"I don't know that it's a trap," Raine repeated. "If Ingrid doesn't sense Skye, then it's possible that the two will obtain the stone through stealth alone. But if Ingrid can sense Skye, it's possible that through magical means she can also see her coming."

"So, you'll just stand here and take that chance?" Dallan said.

"Of course not," Raine replied, rolling her eyes. "We're going that way." She pointed to the other side of the lake, the route opposite that which Skye and Syn had taken.

"Ah," Dallan said with the beginnings of understanding.

"We'll have to make a wider circle," Raine said, "and remain some distance away. If Syn and Skye are undiscovered, we'll do nothing. But if they're found out, then we'll charge in."

"And if we're too late?" Rika asked.

"We'll be too late for the stone," Raine said, "because Ingrid will destroy it. But the sorceress doesn't want Skye dead."

"But what of Syn? And what if the sorceress takes Skye like she took her the first time?"

"The answer to both those questions lies with Syn," Raine said, "because she has certain 'charms' of her own that I'm counting on."

Neither Dallan nor Rika was completely satisfied with this response because they did not know Syn that well. But they trusted Raine more than any other person in Arianthem, so they started off after her through the forest.

Syn and Skye sat crouched in the shadow of the tower, hidden between two walls and behind a stack of barrels. Skye was pleased that Syn had boldly moved so close to the structure, and pleased that they were now so well-hidden, even better than the vantage point from which Syn had analyzed the layout for nearly half an hour. Skye was gaining a newfound appreciation for Syn's skills. Although the thief was ill-at-ease in the forest, she had undergone a startling transformation once in sight of the man-made structure. Skye wondered if Syn had the potential to be as good a scout in nature as the city. Skye's skills translated well even in urban environments, so perhaps it was Syn's past experience and not a lack of skill which made her so uncomfortable in the forest.

The tower was surrounded by an open area, an open area that they had already crossed without incident. This area was patrolled by soldiers and Skye saw with disdain that they were Garmlain. The Garmlain were a greedy and corrupt people that had manipulated the Ha'kan and Tavinter into war against one another simply so they could secure profitable trade routes.

Well, not entirely for the trade routes, Skye reminded herself. For reasons still unknown to her, the Garmlain chancellor had hated her. And he had enlisted the help of the sorceress, Ingrid, who also had some strange, obsessive interest in her. The two had gone to great lengths to nearly destroy the Tavinter and it had only been because of Skye's leadership that the Tavinter had survived at all. Once the Ha'kan had discovered the Garmlain plot, they had turned their army about and crushed the Garmlain in retaliation for their deception.

And now, Skye mused as she stared up at the tower, she was about to walk right into the grasp of that sorceress, the one who had tortured her and most likely had killed her father. She glanced to Syn and chastised herself. Syn's parents had been killed by Hyr'rok'kin, yet here she was coolly assessing the tower like a professional. Skye smiled. The next time she needed to hang a severed head in front of an enemy's dining room window, she wanted Syn with her.

Syn caught the smile out of the corner of her eye and raised an eyebrow in question, but Skye just shook her head. Syn was really beginning to like the young woman because in a way, Skye was as reckless as she was, just far more disciplined about channeling it. Syn pointed up to a window high on the tower, then traced an imaginary path down the side. Skye had taught her some rudimentary hand signals that her people used exclusively when they needed to be silent. Syn did not know enough to go without speech entirely, but it would cut down considerably on the need for conversation.

The imaginary path met with Skye's approval, and she nodded. It would have been her first choice as well. She pointed at the sun, then made the sign for "shadow," and Syn nodded vigorously. In a few moments, the sun would move behind the tower and leave their upward path in darkness. That way, even if the guards looked up, they would not see them.

Skye made the hand signal for rope with a quizzical glance, and Syn shook her head. They could pull back into the crevice that ran vertically down the tower next to their imaginary path if need be, but a rope would hang outward from the parapet and dangle in plain sight. Syn thought long-and-hard, but she didn't have the sign for what she needed to say, so she decided to improvise. She pointed at Skye, then at herself, then held two fingers of each hand pointed downward so each hand looked like a little person. She then stacked one person on top of the other, one after the other, and Skye had to cover her mouth to keep from laughing at the pantomime. She looked up to the imaginary path and saw that Syn was right. The distance between each ledge was such that one could boost the other, then pull the other up. It would not be possible with just one, even jumping, but with two it could be done. Skye again nodded her approval.

The entire time they had been silently devising their plan, both had been memorizing the patterns of the guards. So, they needed no words and no signals for them to know when it was time to move. In perfect coordination, they exited their hiding place and moved hurriedly but quietly across the expanse between them and the building. Once there, they pressed against the stone in shadow, re-assessing the guards, but no one had noticed anything. Then slowly but surely, the two began to climb upward.

The bathwater was luxuriously warm, almost hot, yet still it did not put the sorceress at ease. Something was wrong; she could feel it. Something was near; she could sense it. But she could not identify the source of either feeling or even if the source of the two misgivings was one-and-the-same. She rose from the bath and walked to the full-length mirror, admiring her naked reflection. The blonde hair she had worn as a disguise was gone, replaced with the pure white hair that was hers by nature. Her skin was alabaster white, smooth with no sign of age. Her breasts were large but firm, defying gravity, the pink tips rising at the pleasure of her inspection. The paleness of her coloring was offset by the blue eyes that held such self-admiration. It was amazing what the blood of innocents could do to counteract the effects of time.

Ingrid pulled on a blue robe, one that complimented her eyes, and sat down before her nightstand and a smaller mirror. She combed her hair, unable to shake the feeling of disquiet. She reached down inside her robe to the hidden pocket that was sewn on the interior. She removed the milky stone, stared deeply into the enchanted item, and wondered what was happening to its companion stones. As always, she returned the stone to the pocket for safe keeping, unwilling to separate it from her person. She stood and left the room.

Skye watched the woman from her perch on the ledge outside the window and her jaw worked furiously. She had underestimated the impact of seeing the sorceress again. Everything the woman had done to her came rushing back, how she had imprisoned her and tied her spread-eagle to an altar, carefully hiding her nudity from her other captor, the Chancellor, but opening her robe when she sought to feed. And fed she had, taking her blood in a myriad of perverse ways, violating Skye mind, body, and soul.

Syn's jaw, on the other hand, had dropped. She was greatly disappointed when the sorceress put her robe on because, by the gods, that woman was built. Those breasts, that creamy white skin, those long legs, that white hair on top of her head and then the soft patch of white lower. It made Syn want to put the sorceress on her back and torture her with every skill she had at her disposal.

She became aware that Skye was looking at her with enormous disapproval, and her jaw clamped shut. Focus, she chastised herself, now was not the time to be distracted by breasts. She sent Skye a questioning sign, querying her if they should enter, and Skye nodded with resignation. With expert skill, Syn went through the window and dropped noiselessly to the floor, followed by her stealthy Tavinter companion. Syn felt oddly calm while Skye was certain that Ingrid could hear her heart pounding in her chest.

Syn crept down the hallway in which the sorceress had disappeared. She stopped shy of the first doorway, then peered around the opening. The room was empty. She signed "clear" to Skye, then moved to the next doorway, repeating the procedure. This room was also empty. Syn was fairly certain the sorceress was in the room at the end of the hall, and as her ears strained, she thought she heard sounds of movement that indicated she was correct. Even so, she was cautious as she continued down toward the room. When they reached the final doorway and Syn cleared that room as well, she motioned that Skye should stay put. Skye did not like this plan and was not used to lagging behind, but she complied. She was startled when Syn approached the chamber at the end of the hall, peered in, then slipped around the corner and disappeared.

Everything was quiet save the pounding in her chest. Skye did not see how Syn could accomplish such a bold maneuver without being caught. She had not even hesitated but had walked directly into the room that Ingrid was in. As the minutes dragged by in complete silence, all sorts of scenarios raced through Skye's mind. Ingrid had encased Syn in some magical field which was sucking the life force from her. Ingrid had slit Syn's throat the instant she had rounded the corner and she now lay dying in a pool of her own blood, unable to cry out for help. Each imagined scenario grew worse and Syn's situation grew direr with every second of inaction from Skye. She could stand it no longer and, against Syn's direction, began creeping down the hallway toward the light at the end of the hall.

The sorceress sat bolt upright in her chair and Syn inwardly cursed and pulled back into the shadows. Her hand had been inches from its target, the sorceress unaware of her presence. And she did not think she had alerted the woman even though she was but a foot from her. No, the sorceress turned to the doorway, and although there was nothing there, she had a look of disbelief, recognition, and pleasure on her features, the latter which was not pleasant to see.

"Well, well, well," she murmured.

The gnarled roots that had come up through the floorboard twisted and came to life. Syn had thought their presence odd since they were so high up in the tower, but she had not given it much attention. Now it was clear this was no normal tree as the roots stabbed out into the hallway and returned with a wildly struggling Skye. Skye slashed outward with her sword and took one root off, but it grew back instantly while another wrapped itself about her sword arm. Still she fought mightily and was once again able to partially free herself. But another system of roots joined the battle, wrapping themselves about her torso and pinning her arm once more, and soon she was completely restrained. It became obvious her fight was in vain, and she at last went limp in the monstrous limbs, her breathing harsh.

"Hello, little one," Ingrid said, her pleasure evident. She could not quite believe what was before her. "I heard rumor you survived the wraith root," she said, "and I was already planning to make your acquaintance again. And yet here you've delivered yourself to me."

Skye began struggling once more, terrified and angry, but it was as futile as before.

"So, why have you come here?" Ingrid asked curiously.

"I came for revenge," Skye said, but could not meet her eyes. Ingrid stepped forward and took her chin in her hand.

"The Tavinter are terrible at deception," the sorceress said. "That's not why you came." Ingrid dropped the hand. "And you didn't come alone."

Syn stood behind Ingrid as the sorceress spun around. She glanced up and down the lanky frame, examining and assessing her.

"You're not even carrying a weapon, are you?" Ingrid said.

"No," Syn said, "I'm not much of a fighter."

Ingrid's eyes narrowed. "You're not Ha'kan."

"No."

"And not Tavinter."

"No."

"You're not much of anything, are you?"

Syn shook her head. "No," she said with resignation, "not really."

Ingrid was growing amused. Not only was her prize back in her possession, but this rake, this specimen of debauchery, was also proving interesting.

"I know your type," the sorceress said. "You're a con and most likely a thief. You have no morals and few skills. You've probably bedded half the women in Arianthem, bar maids, farm girls, lonely widows, that sort."

Syn looked up at the ceiling. "Yes, a few witches and a couple of elves as well."

The sorceress laughed out loud, and as she did so, her robe slipped partially open, revealing a hint of those lovely breasts. Syn's eyes went magnetically to the cleavage and Ingrid did not move to cover herself. Skye, on the other hand, was silently cursing her companion. Raine had warned her that Syn could get unreliable if distracted. As much as she tried, Syn could not get her gaze back to eye level.

"Do you see something you like?" Ingrid asked. She did not think it necessary but cast a subtle spell on the woman, one that would mildly befuddle her into giving into base desires.

"Yes," Syn said, feeling a little numb. She felt a startling surge of lust and wished she still had the appendage the witch had given her so she could mount this sorceress and bury it in her. The magnitude of the feeling surprised her.

Ingrid let the robe slip a bit more and Syn could now see almost the entire breast, only the enticing nipples still hiding demurely from her view. "You still haven't told me why you're here," Ingrid said.

Syn stepped closer to her, and Ingrid placed her hands on the young woman's hips. The hands slipped up inside her shirt and caressed her skin, fingering the thin scars.

"What is this?" Ingrid said softly, and Syn felt hypnotized.

"I like to be beaten," Syn murmured, and Ingrid gasped with pleasure. This was turning out to be quite an acquisition.

"Hmm," she said, "I can help you with that. But first you must tell me why you're here."

"We came for some bauble," Syn mumbled, suddenly apathetic to their quest.

"Syn!" Skye exclaimed. She was deeply disappointed in her friend.

"Ah," Ingrid said, understanding, "I should have known." She kissed Syn, forcing her tongue into her mouth, and Syn responded passionately while Skye looked on in disgust. "Now get over there and get your clothes off," Ingrid said, nodding to the huge bed against the wall. She leaned toward Skye as Syn numbly obeyed. "I will happily return home with you, my prize. But I may take this one with me, also." She shrugged. "Or I may just kill her when I'm done with her. Either way, I'm going to enjoy bedding her in front of you."

"Can I watch?" Raine said drily.

Ingrid whirled about, stunned, for here in her room was one of the most dangerous creatures in Arianthem and possibly the most dangerous creature of all, at least to her. And the reason why became apparent as Raine reached out touched the monstrous root, and the entire demonic plant shriveled and disappeared into a pile of ash. Ingrid grew very pale for there is nothing more dangerous to a sorceress than one who is completely immune to magic.

Skye collapsed to the floor and came up with her sword in her hand, but that was unnecessary as all of Ingrid's attention was now on Raine. "This is none of your concern, Scinterian. And if your lover is here, it's none of hers, either."

"Trust me," Raine said, "you would know if Talan were here."

Ingrid's expression grew calculating. "And why exactly are you here?" She removed the glowing stone from her pocket. "I'm guessing you came for this."

Raine looked at the softly glowing gem and sighed in resignation. This had been exactly what she had feared. She might have gotten as close to the sorceress as she was now on her own, but Ingrid was powerful and conniving, and the witch would have held her at bay with the threat of the stone's destruction.

"We could make a trade," Ingrid suggested. Her eyes flicked to Skye. "You know that one belongs to me, that by right, she's mine."

Raine was calm, knowing the consequences of her words. "I think if you look closer, you'll see that she does in fact belong to me."

And it was then that Ingrid saw to what Raine referred, the thin filament of miasma that bound the two, the connection that Raine created when she stood before the gates of the Underworld while Skye vacillated between life and death. It was an unbreakable cord that bound them together, and it did indeed mean that Raine decided Skye's fate.

"Fine," Ingrid said bitterly, "then you'll not get what you want, either."

Skye lunged toward her, but it was too late and with a petulant look, Ingrid crushed the stone in her hand. Raine's disappointment was obvious. Ingrid whirled on Skye, took a step toward her, then stopped. She would not challenge Raine.

"Don't think this is over," Ingrid said to Skye menacingly. "I will find you again," she glanced dismissively over her shoulder, "sometime when your keeper is not on duty. And I'll make you pay for this and everything else." And with that, the sorceress waved her hand in the air and disappeared.

Skye stared at the wisp of smoke, all that was left of her mortal enemy. Even now she did not understand the sorceress's animosity and obsession with her.

"I'm so sorry, Raine," she said, turning to the blue-eyed warrior.

"For what?" Raine asked.

"Everything was for naught," Skye said. "She destroyed the stone just as you said she would."

Raine turned to Syn, who lay in the bed on her side, propped up on her elbow. "Did you get it?"

Syn smiled wickedly and removed the enchanted stone from her front pocket. "Right here."

Skye stared at her in disbelief. "You picked her pocket when you kissed her!"

"Actually, I swapped it with a fake, which was a little harder than just taking it," Syn said. "So, she destroyed a very good counterfeit. But that kiss-and-steal is one of my better techniques."

"By the gods," Skye said, "I thought you were an idiot, falling for her like that."

"She is a good kisser," Syn mused.

"Ugh," Skye said, disgusted, and both Raine and Syn laughed.

"Where are Rika and Dallan?"

"I told them I had this well in hand, so they're downstairs killing Garmlain. For some reason, they really detest them."

CHAPTER 17

Weynild was waiting for them at the tavern in Trygg. After an incredibly lengthy reunion kiss with Raine that made even the Ha'kan shift from side-to-side, she separated herself just enough from her lover to look to the thief.

"You have something for me?"

Syn removed the small box from her person. Raine had thought it appropriate that Syn be the one to give it to Weynild.

"Yes," Syn said formally, "I believe this completes our contract."

Syn popped open the lid to the small box and Weynild took the glowing gemstone. She glanced to the barkeep who was trying to pretend he was not looking, and she nodded to a long table against the wall. It was beneath the loft overhead and would provide a greater degree of privacy, even though the tavern still belonged entirely to them. She settled at the head of the table and Raine at her right while the others spread out along its length.

Weynild removed a silver circlet from her pocket, one that now held three glowing stones with an empty setting for a fourth. She placed the milky stone Syn had provided her in the empty setting, and a small flash of light resulted. The gemstone attached to the bracelet, completing the set, and the bracelet began to softly glow. Raine released her breath, unaware she had been holding it, and she looked to Weynild with a smile.

"Can I ask you what's special about the bracelet?" Syn asked. These two had gone to a tremendous effort to obtain what appeared to be a very simple item.

"This is a fade bracelet," Weynild explained. "It can render one invisible for brief periods, completely undetectable. It can't be worn for any length of time because it works by placing the wearer between worlds, and the person can become trapped there. It's also dangerous because many creatures inhabit that netherworld, Nifelheim."

Both Syn and Skye marveled at the possibilities in such an artifact. To be stealthy was one thing, but to be invisible? That would be something.

"But why would either of you need such an object?" Skye asked. "It doesn't seem that you need to hide yourselves."

"The Hyr'rok'kin are beginning to return," Raine said. "Their numbers are still small, but we've seen this type of surge before. In a few years, they'll begin vomiting out into our world." She looked to Weynild, "And I have a feeling it'll be far more difficult this time to shut the gates."

"You're talking about the gates to the Underworld," Rika said, recalling the epic poem, "the gates to Hel."

"Yes," Raine said.

Dallan's expression was serious. Her mother, Queen Halla, thought the three of them out on a vacation of sorts. It was her intent to tell the Queen the truth as soon as they returned, but now that became imperative as she was going to have to pass on Raine's words as well. The Ha'kan had made a pact with Talan'alaith'illaria, and it was Dallan's intent to see that her army was prepared, not only to protect her people but also to aid the dragon. She could tell by Rika's expression that her future First General was having the same thoughts.

"But how will a fade bracelet help you?" Skye asked.

"I have a gift of stealth that not even you two possess," Raine said, including Syn with a nod. "I'm immune to magic and can move freely and unseen by those who use magic to detect others. My love, on the other hand, is a most magical creature and shines like a beacon to such beings. In the past, we've had to be apart for long periods because we couldn't travel together."

"Oh," Skye said, "and now you need not be separated. Because Talan can wear the bracelet."

"Yes," Raine said, "and unlike most, there's little in Nifelheim that's a threat to her."

Skye thought this marvelous and was more impressed by its romantic implications than those more practical.

"I don't know about you," Syn said, "but I could use a drink." She stood up and walked to the bar while Skye's thoughts continued along a slightly different path.

"So, I belong to you?" she said with a sideways glance at Raine, and a pair of golden eyes swiveled around to her.

"Not that way, little one," Weynild said, and Skye blushed.

"You're connected to me," Raine explained. "It was necessary to save your life. Your fate will always be bound to mine." Syn returned with a round of drinks, all of which were gratefully received, then returned to the bar to retrieve her own. Raine took a long drink from her tankard. "And you should be thankful you don't belong to me in such a fashion," Raine said, nodding to Weynild, "for you would belong to her as well."

Skye swirled the liquid in her tankard. "That wouldn't be so bad," she said under her breath, and the golden eyes swiveled about again.

Raine laughed out loud. "I swear she's more Ha'kan than the two of you."

"We've often thought the same thing," Dallan agreed, and Skye blushed again. Her discomfort caused her to spill a bit of drink down her front, which she looked at with mild angst. "I'm going to go upstairs and change my shirt."

"Let me know if you need help," Rika called after her as Skye disappeared.

Syn took a large swig of her drink, then topped it off again. No sense in having to make two trips. She turned toward the table but a figure in the doorway caught her eye. She stepped toward it, intending to shoo the person away, then stopped in her tracks.

A pair of blue-green eyes glared at her and despite the icy fury in their depths, Syn could not help but marvel at how lovely they were. She drank in the sight of the woman, overjoyed to see her although it did seem odd that the usual elegant gown had been replaced by leather armor. Dallan also saw the figure and got to her feet, but Weynild's commanding tone stopped her.

"Hold," she said. She examined the woman in the doorway, then Syn's pronounced reaction to her. "Why do I have the feeling this might be the Lady Jorden?" she said wryly.

Raine leaned her chair back against the wall. "She looks a bit different than I imagined."

Rika also leaned back against the wall, unconsciously mirroring Raine. "And I've seen that look many times from non-Ha'kan women. Poor Syn," she said, entertained by the unfolding drama.

"That's a different look for you," Syn said dumbly, still trying to grasp that Jorden was there. Her words were entirely too casual for Jorden's liking.

"You!" Jorden exploded. "You liar! I knew that was some story you made up in that note. And here I find you drinking in some tavern with a bunch of women!"

"Wait!" Syn exclaimed, holding up her hands, but Jorden would hear none of it. She picked up a wooden tray and threw it at Syn, who was barely able to block it. Her tankard went flying and sprayed mead all over the wall. The barkeep frowned and glanced over at the table where Raine was seated. Raine removed a pouch of gold from her waist and without looking, tossed it to the tavern owner. He hefted the weight, peered into the bag, then shrugged. If these women wanted to demolish his tavern, they had paid for it. He sat down himself to watch the show.

Jorden picked up two plates and hurled them one after the other at Syn. Syn was able to block the first, but the second grazed her head.

"So, you got what you wanted, and you left!" Jorden said angrily, "Just like you always do. And you had the nerve to leave that stupid note. 'A job,'" she said sarcastically, "and just what kind of job are you on?"

"Wait!" Syn exclaimed, dodging the ladle that nearly took off her head. "You don't understand!"

"If these were Ha'kan," Dallan said, taking a sip of her drink, "they would simply have sex to deal with this."

Raine cleared her throat. "Well, that is where this will lead to, it's just taking a more convoluted path," she said, eliciting a low, throaty chuckle from Weynild.

"I repeat," Rika said with a frown, "I don't understand non-Ha'kan women."

"Did you laugh as you climbed out my window?" Jorden demanded, then picked up a chair. Raine winced as the chair landed. Fortunately, it did not appear well-made and broke into pieces over Syn's upraised arms.

"I feel like I should help her," Raine said, crossing her arms over her chest, "but this is too enjoyable to watch."

"No!" Syn exclaimed. "I told you I had one last job I had to finish!"

"Really," Jorden said sarcastically, "a couple of bar maids to service? A farm girl to violate? You're such a liar."

"I'm not lying!" Syn said, her anger finally rising to Jorden's level. "You think you know when I'm lying. But you don't. I've lied to you before and you didn't know it."

"And when was that?" Jorden said icily, "When did you lie to me?"

Syn's jaw worked furiously but her anger dissipated. She was reluctant to speak, and her audience leaned forward. "I lied when I told you I wasn't falling in love with you," Syn said quietly.

"And there it is," Raine murmured.

"You love me?" Jorden said, taken aback.

"Yes," Syn said almost angrily. "And as many women as I've lied to or seduced or tricked into my bed, I've never done so with those words."

Jorden was silent. Out of everything she expected to come out of the thief's mouth, that had not been on the list.

Just then, Skye rejoined the group and took a seat next to Raine. When the commotion started, she had peered over the top of the stairs to see what was happening, but the relaxed and amused demeanor of her companions told her it was nothing to be concerned about. It appeared that Syn was getting the worst from some woman, but given her reputation, that was not surprising.

"Poor Syn," Raine said, "a bounty from the Empire, a bounty from the Guild of Thieves, and now an angry lover."

Skye took a drink from her tankard, more careful this time. "I can't help her with her lover or the Empire, but I can help her with the Guild."

"How so?" Raine asked, curious. Skye was still carefully maneuvering her drink.

"When the Tavinter were at war with the Ha'kan," she said absently, "we had to steal everything in sight to keep going. I made excellent connections with the Guild because they were the only ones capable of fencing such a large quantity of goods. I know Lagmann personally."

"Then you could get him to remove Syn's bounty," Raine suggested.

Skye laughed. "Yes, probably, but that's a popular misconception."

"What is?"

Skye grinned. "Lagmann's not a man. Lagmann is a woman."

Raine and Weynild looked at one another and the silver-haired woman just shook her head.

"In fact," Skye said, her brow wrinkling as she leaned forward, finally recognizing one of the participants of the brawl, "that's Lagmann right there."

"Your thief is possibly the most unlucky person in all of Arianthem," Weynild said under her breath, and Raine silently agreed.

"So, you don't know me as well as you think," Syn continued, her shoulders slumped. "I was lying then, and I'm telling the truth now. I had one last job to finish. You can ask them," Syn said, waving toward her companions.

Jorden looked to the women lined up against the wall, surprised to see one that she recognized. Perhaps it was Syn's unexpected admission of love, but her usual sharp wit was blunted at the moment.

"Hello Skye," Jorden said.

"Hello Lagmann," Skye said.

Syn glanced at Skye in incomprehension. Why in the world would she call Jorden...?

She whirled back to Jorden and the slumped shoulders came up squarely. "You're Lagmann?"

"And there it goes," Raine murmured.

Jorden had the grace to appear somewhat embarrassed. "Well, I might have told a few lies of my own."

"You're Lagmann?" Syn repeated. "You—, you have hounded me half my life!"

"Well, if you had just joined the Guild when I invited you," Jorden said, as if that explained everything.

"You—!" Syn sputtered. "You're the reason why I have a bounty of a hundred thousand coin on my head!"

"It's a hundred and fifty now," Jorden said uncomfortably.

"What?" Syn said, choking on the word. "It's a wonder I'm not dead!"

"No, I specified you were to be taken alive. I wanted to kill you myself."

Syn looked at her in utter vexation and Jorden had endured enough. She grasped Syn's arms and pulled her to her, wrapping her hands about her waist.

"Look," she said, "I'll remove both bounties from your head, and I won't make you join the Guild. I simply want one thing from you."

"What's that?" Syn said suspiciously, although it felt so good to have Jorden hold her.

"I want you to stop running from me," Jorden said, the blue-green eyes intense. "It feels ridiculous to have to keep my lover under lock and key."

Syn's eyes lowered and her long eyelashes brushed her cheek. "I think I can agree to that," she said with only a trace of stubbornness.

"Good," Jorden said, then kissed her deeply.

"And there it is again," Raine said with satisfaction.

It was several hours before Syn and Jorden reappeared, and this time Jorden was dressed in a lovely blue-green gown that perfectly matched her blue-green eyes. It was a startling transformation and Raine saw how the woman maintained her dual identities so effortlessly.

"Now that is how I pictured her," Raine said as the two reached the bottom of the stairs. Syn had marks about both wrists which Weynild took note of. She was beginning to like the Lady Jorden.

Skye, Dallan, and Rika were all in high humor, partially due to the success of the quest, but also because they had been drinking ever since they had returned. Jorden had not paid much attention to Syn's companions after her initial surprise at seeing Skye, but now she took a good look at them. Syn was indeed running with an interesting crowd. Not only was she accompanied by the undisputed ruler of the Tavinter, Jorden was almost certain the striking young woman with the flashing dark eyes was the Ha'kan Princess, which meant the other Ha'kan accompanying the princess likely possessed an extra-ordinary pedigree as well. She was not certain who the blue-eyed beauty was, but she had a mesmerizing combination of sexuality and danger that swirled about her. And then the last one, the stunning silver-haired woman had a sensuality and power about her that was crushing. And as that gleaming, golden gaze examined her, Jorden noted that the woman's armor was the exact same color as that dragon that had been flying about the duke's castle.

"So, your name is not really Lagmann," Skye said.

"No," Jorden said, "that's a convenient alias, one I use for obvious reasons. And it's much easier to let everyone think Lagmann is a man."

"So, how do you two know one another?" Syn asked curiously, and Skye quickly answered.

"We did some business during the war, when the Tavinter needed funds."

"Ah," Syn said.

The quickness of Skye's response reinforced Jorden's notion that Syn had no idea who her companions were. It was endearing that her little thief was running about with some of the most powerful people in Arianthem and was completely oblivious to that fact.

"Do you have any more of those wonderful accoutrements you passed on to me?" Jorden asked Skye.

It took Syn a moment to realize Jorden was referring to the sexual toys the Ha'kan were so famous for. She stood behind Jorden, shaking her head vigorously, causing Jorden to glance over her shoulder with a raised eyebrow at which time Syn's head motion stopped abruptly.

Skye frowned at Syn. "'Tis for your own good," she said, and Dallan and Rika laughed.

Something caught Skye's eye and she leaned forward. "Jorden, where did you get that locket?"

Jorden touched the locket nestled between her breasts. "It belongs to Syn. It was her mother's."

Skye wrinkled her brow. "May I see it?"

"Of course," Jorden said, and removed the necklace. She passed it across the table to Skye, who examined it at length.

"This is Tavinter," she said at last, "I'm certain of it." She looked up at Syn. "Were your parents Tavinter?"

"I have no idea," Syn said. "Their deaths were so traumatic I remember nothing of my life before the Hyr'rok'kin killed them."

A slow smiled spread across Skye's face. "It's true, then."

"What's true?" Raine asked.

"The Tavinter are closely bound as a people, so our skills and stealth are used for a common purpose. But there's an old joke, a saying, that without one another, we would all be thieves."

"You think I'm Tavinter?" Syn said doubtfully.

"Actually," Raine said, "that does make a lot of sense. A Tavinter removed from the forest and taken away from her people would wind up exactly like you."

Jorden leaned over and kissed her. "So, not only are you the greatest thief in all of Arianthem, you may be a Tavinter as well."

162

Syn marveled at the possibility. She had run from everything her entire life, and now suddenly she had a love, she had friends, and she might very well have a people.

"Do you think the Tavinter would accept me?" Syn asked, and Jorden hid a smile. That heartfelt question confirmed that Syn had no idea whom she was talking to.

"I think I might be able to help with that," Skye said vaguely, and everyone burst into laughter.

Weynild took Raine's hand. "It's time, my love." She stood and turned to Syn. "As promised, I owe you a favor that you may use at any time."

"I feel as if I owe the two of you a favor," Syn said. "I couldn't guess that my life would change this much from a few months ago when I broke into your cottage."

"I'm glad you feel that way," Weynild said, her golden eyes gleaming, "for I may have need of your skills again in the near future."

"I'm at your service," Syn said.

Raine patted Skye, Dallan, and Rika on the shoulders. "I'll see all of you again, soon." She turned to Dallan. "Tell your mother to expect the Alfar," and Dallan nodded. Raine winked at Jorden. "Don't let her run on you, because if she is Tavinter, no one runs faster."

"She'll have a hard time running if she's tied to my bedpost," Jorden replied as Syn blushed. And Weynild decided she was indeed beginning to like the Lady Jorden.

CHAPTER 18

The sorceress stood before the portal, uneasy. What she was about to attempt almost always ended in death. But her desire for revenge was so immense she was willing to tempt the anger of the gods themselves. And the goddess she was about to tempt was perhaps the most dangerous of all.

She spoke the words, ancient, guttural, arcane words of angry supplication. Nothing happened, and Ingrid was both disappointed and relieved. She had convinced herself of the foolishness of such an endeavor when the air in front of her took on an oily, yellowish cast and began to twist and curl about in a wispy, smoky vortex. Appendages began to form within the yellow smoke: arms, legs, hands, fingers, breasts, disembodied sexual organs, and the appendages begin to writhe about as the creature pleasured and tortured itself. Ingrid took a step backward. As degenerate as she was, the sight of the Membrane affected even her. The creature was an amalgam of souls stolen from those it had seduced, absorbing the hapless victims into a carnal hell for all eternity.

A face began to form within the Membrane, a ravishingly beautiful, terrifyingly evil face. Ingrid had to force herself to remain still. The face opened its eyes and they were a dark red, so dark they were almost black, and the vertically slit pupils could barely be seen. The expression on the face was cold with a trace of fury, and the limbs of the Membrane whipped about in a frenzied response, quickening the perpetual, painful orgasm it endured.

"Who dares summon me?" Hel asked imperiously.

Ingrid went to her knees. "Forgive me, your Majesty," she said, then hurried on before the goddess could kill her, "I have a gift for you."

Hel's disdain was evident, but her interest was piqued enough to briefly stay her hand.

"And what could someone like you possibly offer me?"

"I have word on one you seek vengeance against."

Hel laughed and it was a horrible sound, like the rattling of bones. "You have only words for me? I suggest you speak them quickly before I add you to this creature that writhes before you."

Ingrid swallowed hard. The threat of the Membrane was horrifying. "It regards Talan'alaith'illaria."

The Membrane grew still and the face within grew composed. Ingrid had clearly gotten the goddess's attention. "Speak," she commanded.

"I believe the dragon has obtained a fade bracelet."

Ingrid had relived the humiliating confrontation with the dragon's lover numerous times, and it did not take much for her to realize she had been deceived and the stone stolen.

It grew very quiet while Hel contemplated this revelation. This was indeed valuable information. With such a bracelet, Talan could move about Nifelheim nearly undetected. Undetected, of course, unless Hel knew to look for her, because after all, Nifelheim belonged to her.

"I see," Hel said, "then I will allow you to live despite your arrogance in summoning me."

Against her better judgment, Ingrid pressed forward. "I have a proposal for you."

The sorceress was certain she was about to be killed in a most heinous manner, or absorbed right into the mass of writhing filmy flesh. "I can deliver the Arlanian to you," she said, expelling the declaration in one quick burst.

Now Hel's attention was completely on the white-haired woman before her. The dragon's lover was a mystery to most. Some knew that Raine was Scinterian; even fewer knew she was Arlanian. Very few knew that she was both, an impossibility stemming from an improbable union between two very different races. The Scinterians were originally dragon slayers before becoming the inseparable allies of their dragon brethren. The Arlanians, on the other hand, were a gentle race of people so sexually desirable they were annihilated almost immediately upon discovery, forced into a humiliating and degrading slavery and then driven to extinction. None were thought to survive from either mythic race.

Except Talan's lover, Hel thought, the one who made her insides twist with desire. Hel had bedded Arlanians centuries before and the fragile creatures had satisfied her as none other. Unfortunately, not one had survived the act. Hel could not imagine a hybrid with the indestructibility of a Scinterian and the staggering sexuality of an Arlanian. And it infuriated her that Talan possessed such a creature.

"I'm listening," Hel said.

"The Arlanian has intertwined her fate with the one I seek," Ingrid said.

"You speak of Isleif's line," Hel said with amusement, "the one you feel should have been your own." Ingrid glowered with anger as Hel continued. "I find it perverse and enjoyable that you violate the girl simply because she's not your great-grandchild."

A retort died on Ingrid's lips, for she felt the goddess of the Underworld had just as personal a grudge against Talan. But she was thankful to be standing whole and intact, not a pile of ash on the floor or worse, a compilation of body parts joined with thousands of others.

"Regardless of my motives," Ingrid said, trying to regain some dignity, "the girl's blood is powerful," her eyes gleamed as she recalled the taste, "and serves my purposes."

"Yes," Hel said smoothly, "I don't imagine poor Isleif has aged as well as you?"

Ingrid sought to return the conversation to her proposal. "For whatever reason, the dragon's lover took it upon herself to pull the girl, Skye, back from death. In doing so, she created a connection between her and the girl, a connection that might prove a weakness, one that could be exploited."

Hel was thoughtful, and the possibilities inherent in the words of the sorceress were numerous. She would have to give the entire situation much consideration. To strike at Talan and simultaneously enslave her lover, now that would be epic revenge.

"I will consider your proposal," Hel said, then disappeared.

Ingrid fell back, exhausted. The contact with the goddess of the Underworld had left her exhilarated and drained.

CHAPTER 19

Raine stretched in the pile of furs, then rolled over into her lover's embrace. The mountain keep was possibly her favorite place in all of Arianthem, the cave where she had first met Weynild decades before. It was rocky and spare with little more than a fire pit to take the chill from the mountain air and a bed that served the same purpose in different ways. The bed looked out over a lake that was formed when rain pooled from the gigantic opening in the ceiling high overhead. It was accessible only two ways: one, by a death-defying, life-threatening, enormously lengthy and strenuous climb, or second, by flight. The former Raine had done only once as ever since she had returned upon Weynild's back while she was in dragon's form. And that generally meant that they went immediately to the bed upon arrival because riding upon Weynild's sinuous neck was one of most sensual things Raine had ever experienced.

"Might we stay for a while before we head out on some other adventure?" Raine asked, tracing her finger over Weynild's taut stomach.

The dragon watched her lover play with her, again marveling that she had ever found one capable of matching the lust of her kind. Most would require a lengthy recovery after intercourse with a dragon, if they even managed to survive. Her Arlanian, however, could sustain their passion for days. She felt her desire stir as Raine's eyes transitioned to a deep violet, the color of her mother's people, the color that only displayed when she allowed it to, or involuntarily when she was feeling profound emotion. Both situations were true at the moment with the exception that in the latter, the emotion was deep, but the display was voluntary. Raine loved Talan'alaith'illaria with all her heart and all her soul.

"I think we have something of a respite for the time being," Weynild said.

Raine's eyes drifted to the softly glowing bracelet that lay on a rock next to them. "And you're committed to this course of action?"

"Yes," Weynild said.

"I still don't grasp the breadth and depth of your plan."

"What do you mean?" Weynild asked, running her fingers over the blue and gold markings on Raine's back.

"You know I could have obtained all three stones myself."

"I know," Weynild said, smiling. "I have no doubt of that. But much has been put in play by doing it this way."

"I'll take your word on that," Raine said, gasping at the sensation on her back. The markings were extraordinarily sensitive

Weynild maneuvered Raine so that she was face down, then laid on top of her, kissing the back of her neck and her hair while continuing to stroke the markings.

"What are you doing back there?" Raine murmured into the pile of furs.

"What do you think I'm doing?" Weynild said softly, amused, then took her exactly as a dragon would.

ALSO BY SAMANTHA

Scan to see the series!

THE CHRONICLES OF ARIANTHEM

2nd CHRONICLES OF ARIANTHEM

THE DRAGON'S NIGHT (Book 9)
THE SCINTERIAN'S DREAM (Book 10)
THE RISE OF THE SINISTER (Book 11)

visit us on the web at

arianthem.com

follow us on Facebook

ABOUT THE AUTHOR

S AMANTHA SABIAN, author of the "Chronicles of Arianthem" series, enjoys writing about strong, sexy women. Not content simply to tell stories, she creates *worlds*. Her irreverent sense of humor often spills out of the mouths of her characters, who come alive in these remarkable fantasy settings.

Samantha lives in Southern California where she happily spends her day working out, attending art school, and of course, writing. She lives with a cacophony of parrots (more appropriate than "flock"), whose personalities find their way into her books, usually in the form of bossy little dragons.

Samantha tries to answer all email, so drop her a note:

Samantha@arianthem.com

www.ingramcontent.com/pod-product-compliance
Lightning Source LLC
Chambersburg PA
CBHW072122170626
46813CB00004B/1660